For Edward, my first Cyrano

panache   n.1) plume/feather worn in
               a hat or helmet

        2) swagger, style, bravura

Th   in
sm   ed
wit   in
lov   ul
wo

We   nd
Cy   ve
all   al
to

Th   1e
Cy   ch
th   1e
po

CYRANO

From the play by Edmond Rostan

Geraldine McCaughrean

*For anyone who's ever been
hopelessly in love*

First published in 2006 by
Oxford University Press
This Large Print edition published by
BBC Audiobooks by arrangement with
Oxford University Press 2006

ISBN 10: 1 405 661372
ISBN 13: 1 405 661379

British Library Cataloguing in Publication Data available

Printed and bound in Great Britain by
Antony Rowe Ltd., Chippenham, Wiltshire

1

A Night at the Theatre

Who with any sliver of soul in him can resist the sounds, sights and savour of it? That whisper of silk gowns; that hubbub as an audience streams indoors; bores recollecting past plays; fans relishing the play to come; the greetings and insults loosed off like catapults; the flirting, the wagers, the bad jokes, the poets arguing in rhyming couplets ...

See that dizzying cliff-face of boxes decked out in white and gold; the tiered chandeliers being hauled into the roof ablaze with candles; the fleecy bob of wigs and sumptuous swirl of cloaks; the gallants strutting, fingers on sword-hilts; the footlights winking on ...

Feel the jab of saucy elbows, the brush of rouged cheeks as the

1

scandalmongers exchange whispers; the snip-snap of pickpockets dipping like herons into pockets and purses. Countless mouths are already a-glitter with sugar from Monsieur Ragueneau's cream horns. Blushes, drunkenness and rage soak a hundred hatbands with sweat . . . All Paris is crowding into the Théâtre des Muses tonight. Everyone is here—well, with maybe one notable exception . . .

And smell the mouth-watering savour of pasties, éclairs, cloudy claret, and dark tobacco! The tang of oranges, the smarting stench of the limelight, the mixture of sweat and perfume, the aroma of cinnamon and sin. A veritable riot of smells, in fact, vying for the attention of a hundred no—

. . . no, no. No.

Let us not stray on to dangerous ground. There's trouble enough in the world without raising the subject of noses.

The curtain goes up. Silence falls. The evening star is rising in the shape of the magnificent Montfleury! He is as big as a baron of beef and absolutely without talent, but he is very, *very* famous, and isn't that what matters with actors? The audience gives a roar of delight.

*   *   *

The mighty Montfleury had not spoken above three lines when a voice even louder than his own came booming out of the auditorium:

'What? Has this *thing* appeared again tonight?' The audience parted like the Red Sea, and there he stood: Cyrano had come after all. 'Montfleury, I thought I forbade you ever to set foot on stage again! You are the greatest ham since the Gadarene Swine. Be so good as to cart your streaky bacon off the stage and be gone!'

Uproar. Half the audience began to moan and groan, not wanting to be robbed of the play they had come to see. The rest were just as happy to watch Cyrano rant against Bad Acting. Montfleury might be grossly huge and Cyrano as lean as a greyhound, but as

3

celebrities went, Cyrano de Bergerac was by far the larger—larger than Life, in fact.

Montfleury flung his arms about and tried to begin again, but it was hopeless.

'Call yourself an actor? The trees of Birnam Wood were less wooden in *Macbeth*! Will you leave the stage of your own accord or must I cut you up into logs and *burn you*?'

The actor's lines gurgled back down his throat like water down a drain. He could see the white panache on Cyrano's hat looming through the smoke of the footlights, and his two fat little legs told him to run.

The audience took sides:

'Get on with the play!'

'You tell him, Cyrano!'

'Stand your ground, Montfleury!'

'Teach him a lesson, Cyrano!'

But the other actors were protesting on their own behalf. 'Who's going to pay us if we pack up and go home?' they wanted to know. They had no objection to Montfleury-the-Ham getting hamstrung, but they could not afford to lose an evening's pay.

With a flourish worthy of royalty, Cyrano tossed back his cloak, reached across his body . . . *He's going for his sword!'*

. . . and drew out a bulging purse. He tossed it on to the stage where it burst gloriously open, spilling golden coins across the boards and fetching an acrobatic display from the actors as they dived to gather it up. Applause and peals of laughter burst from the gallery: the play might be lost, but the gesture was too impossibly grand to resist. What a divine fool that Cyrano was! What a colossus of style!

Quel panache!

On the sill of a nearby opera-box, however, the fingers of a black-gloved hand drummed irritably. 'The Gascon is making a nuisance of himself,' said the Comte de Guiche, through a yawn of exquisite boredom. 'Do something about him.' One of his retinue slipped out of the opera-box and downstairs to the auditorium.

Cyrano had started to list, in verse, all the reasons for drowning Bad

Actors in big buckets. But he had no sooner started than he was interrupted by a jeering, sneering heckler.

'What's this, then? Is *Sir-run-nose* poking his *nose* in again where it don't belong?'

The crowd gave a gasp. So! The evening's excitements were not over, after all! A foppish young viscount lounged against the edge of the stage, flicking pieces of orange peel around the floor with the tip of his elegant sword, and smirking. 'And such an UGLY nose, too,' he tittered.

A spot of colour touched Cyrano's cheek and he glanced up fleetingly at the gallery. Five hundred pairs of eyes swung to see what he would do next.

After a long silence, even the fop cocked a puzzled eyebrow. 'Well? What are you waiting for? Aren't you going to cross swords with me? I insulted your big fat nose.'

'*You did*? When?'

The fop was wrong-footed. 'I—'

'You call *that* an insult?' Cyrano declaimed. '*Tchtch-tch*. I have trodden in worse insults than that on the

6

pavement. My God, man! If you're going to insult me, at least do it with a little *style*! A little *panache*! Good Lord! There are as many schools of insult as there are tribes of Israel, and is *that* the best you can come up with? I see I must teach you the Art of the Insult!' At last the sword came out—a noise like a snake uncoiling. The onlookers shivered with delicious horror and drew back as far as possible, boys thrust behind their mothers, wives peeping over their husbands' shoulders. Once more Cyrano's grey-brown eyes flickered towards the upper gallery of the theatre and he raised the hilt of his sword to his lips in salute to someone seated there. He did not remove his hat: perhaps he knew that, from up there, its brim concealed his huge beak of a nose.

Then his blade flashed. Fast as the spoke of a carriage wheel it moved. Its reach was as long as a moonbeam. In his hand, it was summer lightning. His voice was calm and very slightly taunting. Such a silence had fallen that his words were audible from the front stalls to the upper gallery.

'ONE! There is the Insult Theatrical. Let me give you an example: *O brave New World that has such noses in it!*

'TWO! There is the Insult Geographical: *Just walking round you is like rounding Cape Horn!*

'THREE! The Insult Inquisitive: *Does it not cause you to tilt over, monsieur, or do you wear counterweights in your boots?'*

The crowd roared with laughter, while the fop roared with frustration, his lunges and parries hitting nothing but the empty air as Cyrano stepped deftly round him.

'FOUR! There is the Insult Punning: *Where does Cyrano come to an end? Nobody nose!*

'FIVE! The Insult Explanatory: *Don't tell me! You grew it that big to keep your feet from getting sunburned!*

'SIX! The Insult Medical: *When you have a cold, monsieur, Belgium floods!*

'SEVEN! The Insult Biblical: *It wasn't Ararat where Noah ran aground, you know?'*

By this time, the gallant had forgotten about sarcastic remarks or showing off or even fencing. He had simply begun to run, lifting his heels higher than his kneecaps as Cyrano carved him clear of the floor.

'You might have attempted EIGHT! The Insult Exaggerational: *Have a care! When you sneeze, whole fleets sink in the Spanish Main!*

'Or NINE! the Insult Unsporting: *You must be the only man who can win a race by a nose before the starter has even fired his gun!*

'Or TEN! The Insult Sentimental: *Aaah! How kind of you, monsieur, to provide a perch for so many ickle squiwwels and birdies!*

'And now—to make an end— The Insult Well-Intentioned: *If you ever lose your scabbard, at least you will always have somewhere to sheath your . . .*' One small flick of his wrist, and Cyrano whipped the foil from his opponent's hand and sent it skidding among the floor rushes. '. . . sword. But no! You aspired to none of these! The words you offered me were about as witty as a dead rat, as clever as a used handkerchief, as original as Thursday!' He leaned forward, as if to dislodge a fly from a cake, and the viscount cowered down, eyes shut, trying to shield the whole of his body with two thin arms. 'So, by your leave, I think I shall not put myself to the trouble of actually *fighting* you, monsieur.' He added coldly: 'The real shame rests with whoever sent you.'

Then Cyrano plunged his sword back into its sheath, leaving the fop gibbering and half-naked amid the rags of his shredded clothing. As the man scrambled and tripped his way out on to the street, he could scarcely believe his luck at getting away alive and unscathed. He wiped his face with relief and found that the tip of his nose was dripping blood delicately on to his lacy shirt. He had been too scared even to feel the nick.

Turning to acknowledge the cheers, Cyrano's grey-brown eyes glanced upwards once more and rested for a fleeting moment on the face in the gallery. His beautiful young cousin reproached him with a shake of her head, but even she could not help smiling at his spectacular, idiotic *coup de théâtre.* Then, in the swish of a silken gown, she was gone, and it was as if one of the great multi-tiered chandeliers had blown out in the draught.

* * *

'Well! Have you made enough enemies for one night?' said his friend le Bret. 'One: Montfleury. Two: the owner of the theatre. Three: that little viscount you shredded. Four ...'

'In that case, my cup runneth over with happiness!' said Cyrano ferociously. 'Everywhere I go, arrogant little jackanapes jump out of the woodwork hoping to get famous by beating Cyrano de Bergerac in a duel. It is tedious in the extreme.'

'You idiot, Cyrano. You'll never get rich if you go about chopping up members of the nobility! And talking of money ... that was a year's pay you threw on stage. What are you going to

11

live on now?'

'I'll manage,' said Cyrano with a shrug. 'Sometimes one single moment is worth a year's pay! Some nights the heart strains at its tethers, doesn't it, and wants to break free and float upwards towards the moon . . .'

'Ah!' murmured le Bret with a smile. 'Do I scent Romance in the air?'

'And you want me to fawn, and lick the boots of men like . . . who? Like that nincompoop? Or men like that black *mole* the Comte de Guiche?' A rictus of loathing crumpled Cyrano's face. 'I've seen him. Eyes like two rabbit droppings. Looking at *her.* He was there tonight. I saw him. Looking at *her.* It was like watching a slug crawl over a rose.'

'Aha! It's true then! I'm right! The great Cyrano, whom no swordsman can fell, has finally fallen prey to Love? Go on, then. Who is she?'

Cyrano smiled a lopsided smile that tugged his great nose to one side like the boom of a yacht. He was full of self-disgust. 'Look at me, le Bret. Who *would* it be? Look at this sundial face of mine! My own mother found me repellent. Who would I fall in love with but the sweetest, most delicate beauty in all France—a girl with such an eye for beauty that Beauty itself rides in the carriage of her eye!'

'Oof,' said le Bret. 'Her. Your little cousin. Roxane. I saw her peeping over the balcony this evening, eyes as big as saucers. Well? Why the long face? Tell her! Declare yourself! Why not?'

Cyrano gave a mirthless bark of laughter. 'Why not? Why not? Me? The only clown who doesn't need make-up to get a laugh? Why not? Because of this, that's why! Because of this . . . this . . . this *extrusion* of a—' He broke off with a gasp akin to pain, one hand masking his face.

Le Bret was appalled. He reached out and touched the man's sleeve. 'Cyrano. My dear friend. Are you . . . crying?'

'Never!' Cyrano snatched his arm away, the offer of sympathy intolerable. 'I never cry! Tears don't suit a gargoyle like me. Tears have no place sliding down this *sledge-run* of a nose! Me, I stay doggedly dry-eyed through any amount of loneli—Anything else would be absurd.' He broke off. 'Roxane, yes. That's her. Roxane.'

For him the name alone held more poetry than the entire *Song of Songs*.

'Oh, Cyrano, you have the soul of a poet,' whispered le Bret. Coming from him, it was the kindest, highest form of praise. For le Bret was himself a poet.

Cyrano made a great effort and shook off melancholy like a dog drying itself. 'Well! And so do you. So do you, le Bret. You haven't exactly been sucking up to the aristocracy lately, I hear. Is it true you've been handing out rude verses again? You'll make one too many enemies yourself one of these days. Why do you do it?'

*'I measured Risk against Truth and
    Truth was longer!
Fear strove with Honour and Honour
    proved stronger!'*

declared le Bret grandly . . . though, truth to tell, he had been growing more and more ashen as the evening wore

14

on. 'Actually, Cyrano . . . I did hear a kind of ugly rumour that there are . . . er . . . a hundred men waiting outside the theatre to cut me in ribbons.'

'In that case, isn't it time you bought a sword?' said Cyrano blithely.

Just then, a skinny little woman tripped into the darkened stalls (an opera mask was making it hard for her to see where she was stepping) and landed at their feet with a noise like a burst football. 'Psst! Message for Monsieur Cyrano!'

'I know you, don't I? You're Roxane's maid!' said Cyrano hauling her to her feet. (His other hand he put to his chest as if to hold his heart in place.) 'You have a message from my cousin? For *me*?'

'Yes! My mistress would speak with you, sir. Alone. Somewhere public but private, if you know what I mean.'

'Alone? Me?' The great booming voice that had shaken Montfleury off the Paris stage shrank suddenly to a dry whisper. Cyrano swallowed, cooled his face with the cuff of his shirt, his great nose momentarily hidden from sight

15

amid the lace.

'Tomorrow at noon at Ragueneau's pastry shop. You will come, monsieur, won't you?' the maid begged, jerking her sharp little face upwards at his, but managing to reach only his chest. 'From the pallor of my lady's face, it is surely a matter of the heart!'

Dumbly Cyrano nodded, eyes wide with something like fear. The maid stumbled out again and collided with an orange-seller.

'Aha! A rendezvous! A tryst?' exclaimed le Bret with a grin. 'Whatever can it mean?'

'That I am not invisible,' whispered Cyrano to himself, breathless with astonishment. 'That she has seen me. That she . . .' Like the spilled oranges bouncing down the aisle of the theatre, Cyrano's heartbeats tumbled through him, golden, sweet, falling bruisingly hard.

And then such a torrent of hope and energy swept over him that he needed to run, to fight, to dare, to leap, to swallow down the moon! He grabbed le Bret by the front of his scruffy jacket.

'A hundred assassins, did you say? Coming to chop you up?'

'I thought I'd maybe hide in the storm drain till they've gone,' said le Bret beginning to wilt at the knees. 'Then leave the country.'

'Rubbish, man!' cried Cyrano leaping on to the empty stage and ripping the smoky air to smuts with a slash of his sword. 'Let them all come! I shall fight them on your behalf! I shall pollard them like willow trees! I shall prune them like Hercules slaying the hundred-headed Hydra! I shall pluck them like the petals of a *daisy—sheloves-me-she-loves-me-not—* and send them back to their paymaster to wear as curlers in his wig! Come on, man! Let's give the moon something to watch! Let's be meteors and blaze our names in the sky! Life is rapture . . . and tonight I am a hundred men in one!'

17

2

A Hundred Against One

Perhaps it was not quite as many as a hundred: poets do tend to exaggerate. But on a dark night, on wet and unlit streets, with the night-watch bribed to stay away and God-fearing citizens all at home in their beds, there were quite enough assassins to dispatch one little unarmed scribbler.

As le Bret and Cyrano left the theatre, dark figures stepped from every alley and doorway, dropped from the eaves of houses and the tailgates of carts. They padded like cats on the prowl, but instead of the glint of green eyes, there was the ting of metal, the dull flicker of starlit steel. Now and then an oath was dropped, like rotten fruit, as one of the assassins trod in horse dung or twisted his ankle on the cobbles. They were dressed all in black.

It is hard to count black-clad men on a moonless night. Perhaps there were a hundred after all.

Le Bret slithered into the storm drain and sat there with his eyes tightly shut, while leather-soled boots closed in on all sides: rats converging on a carcass.

There was one streak of whiteness amid the black: a white ostrich feather topping a broad-brimmed hat. Curling and uncurling in the rain, it looked like a finger beckoning the assassins on.

Then all Hell broke loose.

Some of the bandits said afterwards that le Bret had hired himself a platoon of guards; others that he had summoned up demons from the Underworld. Some blamed a freak wind for robbing them of their swords and tearing the seats out of their trousers. Others admitted they had no idea what hit them.

Cyrano's rapier threaded between them like a needle through tapestry, leaving a strand of red here, a squeal of yellow there. He cut the tassels from their cloaks, the buckles from their boots, the brims from their hats, the cuffs from their gauntlets. Black kerchiefs fluttered down from their startled faces. They lashed and lunged and parried, but seemed only ever to hit brickwork or each other. Soon they were yowling like cats in a dog-pound. The white panache swooped among them—a dove inflicting peace with the aid of an extremely sharp beak.

The poets were still making up verses about it as they mustered at Ragueneau's pastry shop next day. The identity of the lone swordsman was still a mystery, but facts and details never stopped poets immortalizing such things:

'One hundred against one they came,
Their blades as silver as the rain.
Then wished themselves back home
    again
When they met . . . blah blah . . . *in the*
    lane!

Doesn't anyone know yet who it was?'

They went there every day for lunch. Ragueneau was so much in awe of

21

poets, such a sucker for Poetry, that he daily fed them for free on cream cakes and quiche Lorraine. It drove his wife to distraction. She raged and railed at him, slapping at his great round shoulders until the flour flew off him in clouds. 'Time-wasters! Freeloaders! Parasites! Send 'em home! You'd see your own children starve sooner than deny an éclair to some hollow-legged hack of a rhymer! I forbid you to serve 'em! Send 'em home!'

Ragueneau ignored her, much as he ignored the flies circling over his pastries. He continued to beam and bow and trot to and fro serving hot chocolate and sponge fingers to the scruffy assortment of scroungers lounging along the bench-seats. Madame Ragueneau took her revenge. She went to his desk and folded up all his own lovingly penned attempts at poetry and turned them into paper-bags for the shop. When Ragueneau realized that he was shovelling apple tarts, crêpes, and choux buns into cones made of 'Chloe's Wedding' and 'Orpheus' Lament' he let out a wail of sorrow and began chasing after customers, plying them with free cakes and begging them to give him back the bags.

The poets meanwhile simply went on munching, arguing, and looking for words that rhymed with 'assassins' or 'moonless' or 'anonymous'. They barely looked up from their meringues when the anonymous subject of their poems strode through the shop, head down, and disappeared into the room at the back of the shop. Cyrano looked like a man walking over volcanic lava.

He was an hour early. For fear of being late, he was an hour early, and for him the minutes crawled by like snails. 'Is it nearly twelve, Ragueneau?'

'Just turned eleven, monsieur.'

'What time is it now, Ragueneau?'

'Ten past eleven, friend.'

A minute or two more and Cyrano knew it was impossible—that he could no more keep a rendezvous with Roxane than swallow fire. How could he stand face-to-face with her and declare his love—whatever she herself thought of him?

'What time is it now, Ragueneau?'

'Twenty past eleven, friend.' Ragueneau wiped the jam off 'An Ode to Fondant Icing' and tried to flatten the crumples out of the ruined masterpiece.

What if Cyrano were to write his feelings down? Yes! Then all he had to do was put the letter into Roxane's hand when she arrived, and slip silently away! It would hardly take long: this particular love letter had been writing itself inside his head for years. It would be just like copying it off the lining of his eyelids. Cyrano sat down and began to work.

A few minutes later, Roxane and her maid arrived, startling Cyrano who was deeply engrossed. He snatched up the paper off the flour-dusty tabletop and crammed it into his pocket.

'Roxane.'

'Cousin.'

For an eternity, the three of them stood looking at one another.

'Do you like cream puffs?' said Cyrano, pouncing ferociously at the maid.

'Oh! To distraction, sir!'

Cyrano grabbed three empty cones of paper and began to fill them with the cakes and pastries cooling on racks on the kitchen table. 'Éclairs? Macaroons? Strudel?' The maid nodded, her eyes glistening with joy. 'Take them! Take these . . . these green marzipan things, whatever they are. Take them outside, walk up and down And don't come back until you've eaten every last one.' The maid blinked and nodded as best she could while balancing three parcels of cake between both hands and her little pointy chin. Cyrano hustled her outside amid a cloud of icing sugar, then softly closed the door again. He left his face towards the woodwork. 'Roxane.'

'Cyrano.'

'You wanted to see me. I am indebted to you—for calling me to mind, I mean. Anything I can do to be of . . . You know that. Anything I can ever . . . You only have to say . . .' He broke off, his throat tight with terror at the power this young woman wielded over him; the gift of happiness she could bestow or withhold.

'Oh, cousin!' exclaimed Roxane, cheeks colouring as if an oven door had opened nearby. 'I think my whole future happiness may rest in your hands!'

'Oh!'

'You won't think me immodest? If I open the secrets of my heart to you? If I speak of . . . of a secret passion?'

'No! Oh! No! Oh, God!' The swirling wood-grain of the door imprinted itself on his brain. His heart was tumbling through space into her little hands, into her tender little hands. He would take her fragile beauty into his safekeeping, and she, in return, would allow his heart to roost in Paradise.

'There is . . . a man!'

'Yes?'

'A man in your regiment.'

'Yes?'

'In your very own platoon!'

'Yes?'

'And, oh, Cyrano, he's good and brave and worthy of any amount of love, I know it!'

26

Cyrano spun round to face her. Her eyes were shut in rapture. 'Oh, and he, too . . .'

'And so *beautiful*!'

Cyrano tried to breathe, but his lungs were no more than the empty paper cones someone had crumpled flat. 'Beautiful?'

'I haven't actually spoken to him yet, but no one with a face like his could be anything but marvellous and good! His soul shines out through his eyes!'

Cyrano held a hand up to his face. On the wall beside him, his shadow seemed to thumb its prodigious nose at him. Cyrano the fool. Cyrano the absurd. Cyrano the ludicrous, misbegotten clown. His tumbling heart struck the floor and broke, unnoticed, like a bird's-egg nudged from its nest by a cuckoo. 'What is his name, this paragon of masculine beauty? Do I know him? I can't quite see where I . . .'

'He's one of your cadets. I saw him at the theatre last night! Our eyes met. It was love at first sight. His name is—' (She spoke it as if biting into

27

honeycomb.) 'Christian de Neuvillette.'

Cyrano blinked. A mistake. Some merciful mistake. 'I regret, lady . . . There is no one by that name in the Company of Guards. It's not a Gascon name.'

'He joins tomorrow! And he's not a Gascon, no. Oh, but you will take care of him for me, won't you? You will be a friend to him? I've heard how your boys can torment a newcomer—especially when he's not from Gascony.'

The sky had blown away, leaving only the dark. The planets unthreaded from their spheres and rolled away into blackness. 'It is a small enough favour you ask of me, lady,' said Cyrano.

'But promise me! Promise you won't let any harm come to him!' In her earnest eagerness she rested her hands against his jacket. He wondered, with some curiosity, why the blood from his soul did not stain her fingertips.

'Since you ask it, I shall cherish him as dearly as . . . as this white panache.' So, of course, their two pairs of eyes settled on the white plume in his hatband and he had to turn the hat about and about in his big hands for fear she notice how violently the feather was trembling.

'What a dear friend you've always been to me, cousin!' she exclaimed, and brushed his cheek with her lips. They had known each other since their shared, sunlit Gascon childhoods. Despite that—because of it, probably —Roxane was not even aware of him as a man, as a man made of flesh and blood and passion, as a man whose heart was waning within him now like an old moon.

Outside in the street, the maid crushed the third of the paper cones to death between her sticky hands. Cyrano knew it. He felt it. Respectfully he opened the door to bring the rendezvous to an end. Roxane brushed against him in the doorway. 'Oh, and, Cyrano! For the love of God! If he should if Christian should have anything to say to me . . . on the matter of love, I mean . . . *tell him to write!*'

If, in that theatre, Cyrano de Bergerac (author, soldier, and poet) had thrown on stage a purse containing all the words pent up inside him if they had burst free and rolled, glistening and golden, for everyone to hear . . . then by now all Paris would have been wading knee-deep in love poetry.

But she wanted *Christian* to write.

Cyrano inclined his head; bowed flamboyantly so that she would not see his eyes. And she was gone.

'For the love of God' did she say? What did God have to do with it?

3

Christian

Outside in the shop, there was the crash of overturning furniture, some shouting, and the trampling jingle of spurred boots. His fellow cadets, from the Company of Guards, were one step ahead of the poets. They had discovered the identity of the hero of 'One Hundred Against One'. They burst into the bakery and ransacked it until they found what they were looking for their prized and renowned Captain Cyrano—and carried him shoulder-high to the inn across the street.

In the absence of a proper war to fight, the cadets loved nothing better than to hear a good account of a fight. The bloodier the better. In the eyes of these boys, Cyrano de Bergerac was the perfect Gascon—insuperable swordsman, sardonic wit, writer of verse, shabby genius. Each one would have gladly lain down and died for him (if it were not that Gascon boys are all immortal). In all France there was no one to match him. With his bowsprit of a nose, he was the flagship of their fleet. In a war of words or blades no one ever got the better of Cyrano!

Oddly enough, the Captain did not seem over-eager to recount his splendid encounter with the hundred assassins. 'Another time. Some other time, perhaps,' he told them, staring into his wine.

One man in the inn held Cyrano in far less esteem than his fellow troopers. 'Ah, de Bergerac,' crooned a nasal, mocking voice. 'All Paris is buzzing with your . . . *exploits* of last night. *Very* impressive, I'm sure.' It was the Comte de Guiche, resplendent in black velvet that soaked up the light like a sponge. 'I hear you write plays, too—and poetry. My, my. I have half a mind to become your patron and make you *my* poet.'

Cyrano rose, put the knuckles of one

hand on his hip, and threw back his head. 'I am my own man, Comte. What I write, I write for the glory of Art!'

'Naturally. And with me as your patron, your plays might *even* get staged. I don't suppose I would want to rewrite them much.'

'Rewrite them? God's teeth. I'd rather throw them in the Seine.'

De Guiche placed his silver-headed cane before him and rested both hands on it, regal as Neptune commanding the waves. 'You are *very* proud, Captain.'

'You are very observant, Comte.'

On to this tense and uneasy scene came a cadet carrying a half dozen big, cockaded hats skewered on the blade. 'Look what I found lying around, out at the back of the theatre, Captain! Some of those partridges and grouse you bagged last night!' The Company of Guards began to celebrate all over again.

'Whoever paid those assassins must really be cursing this morning!' crowed one.

'Maybe the coward will do his own

dirty work next time!' said another.

'Doesn't anyone know who the devil was, yet?'

De Guiche watched them from under lowered lids as they tossed the hats to and fro among their sword points. Then he rapped his cane once on the floor with a noise like a pistol shot. 'That would be me,' he said. 'I sent them. A bad poet deserves a bad end.'

An awkward silence fell.

Handed two 'hat-kebabs' by his men, Cyrano walked over to de Guiche, regarded him for a few moments, then upended the swords, scattering the grimy, crumpled hats into his lap. 'In that case, perhaps you would be good enough to return these to their owners.'

De Guiche rose sharply and called for his sedan chair. 'Write for the sake of Art, do you? Well, Art is welcome to you, de Bergerac,' he sneered. 'But do remember the story of Don Quixote, won't you? Knights who joust with windmills risk getting knocked face-down in the mud.'

Cyrano met his gaze levelly and with the vestige of a smile. 'Or up to the stars, your honour.' Then he bowed extravagantly, and de Guiche departed with as much dignity as his wealth, rank and pomposity allowed him.

*   *   *

Le Bret was livid with his friend. 'Your big chance! He was offering to put your plays on, man! Aargh! When will you ever stop looking gift-horses in the mouth?'

But if le Bret was angry, Cyrano was perfectly seething with rage. 'I'd sooner starve than be a boot-licker to the likes of that *tick*. I hate his kind. I hate his sneering, vicious, condescending, lightless . . .'

'Now, now.' Le Bret reached out a restraining hand and shushed him like a child. 'And where will that get you? Where did hate ever get anyone?'

'It'll keep my neck from bowing to his sort!' hissed Cyrano. 'It'll keep my head high! I'll wear hate like a Spanish ruff to keep my head held high!'

His old friend was not fooled for a moment. Discreetly he passed the captain a handkerchief, and under his breath he murmured: 'You can call it hate till the sky freezes over, Cyrano. The truth is, she doesn't love you. Am I right?'

Cyrano's erect head sank abjectly forward. 'The truth is, she doesn't love me, le Bret.'

'So give us the account of One Hundred Against One! Tell it!' urged the cadets, recovering their high spirits now de Guiche was gone, and bouncing round him like puppies. The captain's smile was half-hearted. He avoided their eyes. It seemed as if he might even refuse again. *'Tell it! Tell it in verse!'* they chanted.

'Oh, my poor Cyrano,' whispered le Bret.

'Shut up!' Le Bret's kindness only doubled his humiliation. Cyrano resolved that never again would he confide his feelings in another human being. He would stitch them up like a seaman's body in a shroud and bury them under swagger and bragging.

'But you had raised your hopes so high, man.'

'Shut up, I said!' And whirling aside from le Bret into the midst of the crowded inn, Cyrano began to declaim:

'Come, sirs, and I will tell you of a fight
In which one man put five-score men to
*   flight!*
In   which   the   single   swordsman
*   (Cyrano)*
Slashed the panaches from one hundred
*   chapeaux!*
It was a damp night and a dangerous
*   place;*
Too dark to see my hand before my . . .'

'Nose?'

A paroxysm of boredom shook Cyrano. Another 'wit'? Another chancer? No, he could not be bothered.

'The only way to count them, thus
*   disguised,*
Was by the evil glinting of their . . .

'Noses?'

One of his fellow cadets this time, damn him! Showing off to the others. No, he would not be bothered.

*'Like swarming rats (their numbers were
    so rife)
And each one with designs upon my . . .'*

'Nose?'

Someone should have warned the boy of the risk he was running. But then perhaps they had put him up to it. Cyrano shouldered his audience aside to find the source of the insults: a blond-curled, smooth-faced youth with long-lashed, large blue eyes like a Persian cat. To Cyrano's surprise, he had never even seen the lad before. 'You picked the wrong day to cross me, pretty boy! What's your name?'

The boy blenched a little but cocked his nose in the air and struck a saucy pose. 'I am Baron Christian de Neuvillette,' he said.

'Then listen here, de Neu— Who?'

So. This was the boy to whom the gods had given everything. These were the blue eyes that had captured hers across a crowded theatre. These were the golden curls that had entangled her heart.

Breathless with anticipation, the cadets waited to see the new boy swatted flat. For the sin of not being a Gascon like them, they had dared the poor sap to do it, and because he was not a Gascon, they did not care how many slices the captain cut him into.

But amazingly nothing happened. No thunder-bolt fell. No blood hit the wall. Cyrano simply pressed on with his account:

'Timing was crucial, as it is in rhyme.
So with utmost care I picked my—'

'Nose?'

                     '. . . time! My time!
There were a mere one hundred, after
   all,
And each of them was heading for . . .'

'Your nose?'
'Out! Everybody OUT!'

39

The room emptied around them. The two remained, confronting each other, sweating in the heat from the fire. Christian de Neuvillette wetted his lips and regretted not making a will.

'She is my cousin, you know.'

'Wh-who is?' stammered de Neuvillette.

'Mademoiselle Robineau. Roxane. She is my cousin. We played together as children.'

'Oh!' (He had at least the good grace to blush at the mention of her name.) 'Oh, sir! Sir! No, I didn't know, sir, no! I'd really like you to know, sir, that that I really, really admire you! Always have! Your panache! Even your plays! Absolutely! Very much! Everything!'

'Even my nose?'

'No! *Yes*! Aah! Sorry! Sorry, sir! It's just that the others dared me to . . .'

'She wishes us to be friends,' Cyrano cut in. De Neuvillette's face was etching itself on his eye: the perfect slopes and inclines of the cheek, the angular jaw, the straight, unimpeachable nose. 'She wishes us to be good friends.' Christian had left his mouth very slightly ajar. It was the only thing that marred his godlike good looks. Cyrano tried to see whether the soul of the man truly shone out of his absurdly blue eyes, but there was too little light in the room: Christian's soul would have to wait until another day.

Outside in the yard the cadets listened ghoulishly for the sound of pain and mayhem. But nothing came: only the low murmur of voices. 'What's happening? What are they *doing*?' One of them climbed up to peer in at the window. What he saw astounded him. For the captain had his arm around the new recruit, and their heads were close in conversation. The peeping-Tom whistled in astonishment and softly called down to the others: 'It must be open season on noses!'

*   *   *

'She wants you to write to her,' said Cyrano. 'To set your feelings down in words.'

'Write?!' Christian could not have been more horrified if Cyrano had

41

suggested eating raw hedgehogs.

'You *can* write, I suppose?'

Christian snorted. 'Well, naturally I can *write*. Joined up and everything! It's just that . . . poems and suchlike? Love letters?' Once again the mouth hung open, and Cyrano thought that he glimpsed, between those perfect white teeth, a space as large as an empty library: a vacancy. 'I don't do words, sir! I'm too stupid. I'm an utter fool!'

'Oh, I wouldn't say that,' said Cyrano magnanimously. 'You waxed reasonably funny on the subject of noses just now.'

Christian winced. 'But Love? Oh no. I mean . . . not without *help*!'

Cyrano let out the strangest sound. It might have come from a drowning man who suddenly sees the possibility of breathing again. He turned his face away and was silent for a long, long time.

'I dare say . . .' he began at last, in an offhand way, 'I dare say I could help.'

'You?'

'Why not? We could combine our qualities, what say? My eloquence and your looks. Could you—I mean just for instance—memorize words to say to her? If I taught them to you ahead of time?'

Christian was bewildered. 'But why should you? What's in it for you?'

Cyrano shrugged nonchalantly. 'The notion appeals to the poet in me. Like wearing a mask. You'd take my words. I'd take on your face. What do you say?'

Christian shook his head. 'But this letter she wants. I mean . . . I just couldn't.'

'Consider it done! In fact—' Like a magician producing an elderly rabbit, Cyrano drew from his pocket a rather crumpled letter. It was the one he had written while waiting at the bakery shop. 'Hey presto! One love letter. Oh, you needn't worry: it's very good.'

Christian still looked doubtful. 'I'm sure! I'm sure! But surely . . . this was written for someone else . . . I mean, will it *fit* Roxane?'

'Like a glove. In every particular. Trust me. And Roxane will believe it was written for her because she wants

43

to believe it. That, my dear collaborator, is the vanity of Love.'

*   *   *

The Company of Guards could hardly believe their eyes when Cyrano de Bergerac and the new recruit emerged from the inn apparently on the best of terms.

'It's getting harder to put the captain's *nose* out of joint!' some wit remarked out loud.

In the next second he found the point of a rapier hovering like a wasp under his nose, strumming the stiff little hairs of his moustache. Then his vision filled up with nose, as Cyrano brought his face up as close as breathing allowed. *'Want to put that to the test, soldier?'*

The entire platoon showed a sudden intense interest in checking their coat buttons, spurs and cuffs and whether their scabbards were hanging just so.

4

Utter Fools

Like starlings roosting at sunset, the letters fluttered into Roxane's life: sometimes single sonnets, sometimes twelve pages of close-written prose told her of her inner and outward perfections. Their language was so full of stars and planets, comets and constellations that reading them was like looking through a telescope. Whole menageries of animals were pressed into the service of simile. Angels and archangels, cherubim and seraphim flew to the cause of Love. Myth and magic, alchemy and astronomy were woven into flying carpets and laid at her feet. In short, the letters Roxane received were beyond her wildest hopes.

Every evening she and Christian would meet in the town square and she would take his arm and they would walk together, up and down, up and down, while Christian spoke words so eloquently sweet that he might almost have learned them out of a book! Before going, she would set the topic for them to discuss next day drama, history, books, paintings . . . Whatever subject she set, his words always came round to love—his love for her so the topic did not greatly matter.

And her cousin, bless him, had been as good as his word! He had taken Christian under his wing, kept him clear of brawls and bullying. In fact the two men seemed to go about everywhere together, the best of friends. Clearly Cyrano could see Christian's qualities for himself. It confirmed what Roxane already knew: that Christian de Neuvillette was Beauty and Goodness made flesh.

Until that night at the theatre, she had simply been waiting for Christian to enter her life.

One day they might even kiss. The prospect was so marvellous that she did nothing to hasten it. The idea of

Christian was like a perfect reflection in a mill pool. She did not want to disturb it by splashing.

*　　　*　　　*

The Comte de Guiche, on the other hand, was a pest.

Whenever she turned round he was there, paying her unwanted compliments, making assumptions. He seemed to think that his great wealth, his high rank, his oily charm gave him a chance of winning her love! In fact he seemed almost to think of her as his already—his private property, his delicious secret.

Unlike Cyrano, Roxane kept her dislike of de Guiche well hidden. He frightened her. There was something about his mole-black smoothness that made the hairs prickle in the nape of her neck. Their conversations were brittle and tricksy. She had the wit to keep her love for Christian secret, too: de Guiche had enough power to snuff out a man's entire career—maybe even his life, some dark night. Better to

flatter and smile—even flirt a little—
rather than anger the spiteful comte or
make him jealous. She was not unduly
worried. Like all beautiful women,
Roxane Robineau knew she wielded
great power. In her happiness, in fact,
she felt like the sun at the centre of the
universe, and quite clever enough to
juggle several planets before breakfast.

'Good evening, Comte! What a
pleasant surprise.'

'Good evening, mademoiselle.
Forgive me calling unannounced, but I
have come to say goodbye,' said de
Guiche.

Here was a pleasant surprise!
'Goodbye, Comte?'

'Yes, the Guards are ordered to join
in the besieging of Arras. I am on my
way to deliver sealed orders to the
commanders of each regiment. Then I
too must go. Say you'll miss me.'

A hundred dark thoughts rushed
into Roxane's head like hired assassins.
The whole army going into action? The
Company of Guards, too? *Christian*?
Blind panic almost got the better of
her. Then she smoothed the creased

48

satin of her dress and smiled blithely. 'That will please my fool of a cousin, ha-ha! Cyrano does so love a war!'

The comte knew very well that Cyrano loved a war. He was banking on it. He fully intended to post the Company of Guards to the most dangerous positions at Arras. With any luck, Cyrano would get himself killed. But that was not the most delicious part of the plot. 'I thought, my dear, that I would see them on their way and then *slip back* to town. Here. To you, my love. Oh, Roxane! Let me! Let me come to you!'

And suddenly he was there, burrowing his nose into her hair, the black fur of his cloak brushing her ankles like a dog, his breath smelling of crystallized flowers. 'Think of it! Nothing and no one to disturb us! All eyes on Arras and no prying eyes left in town. Let me come to you, lady!'

The comte's romantic ambitions were no longer funny. This was rabies in the yard, snapping at her heels. She must think. She must think! 'Oh, but what about your *reputation*, Antoine!'

Roxane gasped, squirming free. 'I couldn't *bear* for you to risk your reputation! Not when you are so *admired* by your men! If they ever found out, they might mistake you for a coward! A dirty little duty-shirking coward . . . not realizing the truth, of course. Oh, Antoine, I couldn't bear that!'

The comte's eyes blinked at her, too close to focus comfortably without pince-nez. 'You never called me Antoine before.'

Roxane forged on. 'And talking of cowardice . . . you've given me a wonderful idea . . . Antoine. If you really want to upset my wretch of a cousin, you should *keep the Gascons back* from the war! Make the Company of Guards kick their heels in Paris after everyone else has gone! You know Cyrano never misses a chance to cover himself in glory. Well, teach him a lesson! Make him eat humble pie for once. Make him watch the other platoons march off to war while the cadets have to stay at home!'

In that moment, Antoine de

Guiche's admiration for Roxane Robineau increased tenfold. He had never realized before that, underneath her demure façade, she had a nature as cunning and conniving as his own. Though a Gascon himself, the sheer unkindness of her idea tempted him, like black liquorice. Humiliate the great Cyrano de Bergerac by not sending him and his hooligan comrades to Arras?

'By God, I'll do it! I will! I'll keep the Gascons back, just to see the look on Cyrano's ugly face! Arras can fall without the help of that insolent clown!' He sniggered. 'Though the sappers could have used that nose of his as a battering ram, ha-ha!'

His own snub nose snuffled once more in her hair, like a pig rootling for truffles. Then he tore himself away. A fistful of letters remained to be delivered to the various platoon commanders, and sometimes even the Comte de Guiche could not escape his obligations.

Roxane Robineau sank down on to her chaise longue until the fright of the moment passed.

Then she congratulated herself on her cleverness and returned to contemplating her favourite topic: Christian.

*   *   *

On her way out to a soirée that evening, she chanced upon Cyrano, who just happened to be passing. Strange how often that seemed to happen lately. Secretly she suspected that the world-weary old cynic enjoyed teasing her about her secret love and sought her out specially to do it. Well, she could tease as well as he!

'And what subject will you set him tonight, your little winged Cupid?' was the first thing Cyrano said.

'Oh, tonight I think I shall simply tell him to improvise on the theme of Love. Whatever he says will be sublime.'

'Good. Excellent. Yes.'

'But don't tell him ahead of time, will you, cousin? I don't want him rehearsing what to say!'

'Perish the thought, mademoiselle.'

Inside the loft of Cyrano's mind the whirling confusion of feelings began to roost and grow calmer. Instantly, he set to work that part of his brain that turned feelings into words and words into wooing. It soothed him so much, this furnishing of words for her pleasure. Just as the tapestry workshops of Arras and Gobelin turned out opulent wall hangings for kings to rest their eyes on, so Cyrano daily produced the quota of words with which Christian de Neuvillette wooed and won Roxane.

'And does he write well, your Dante, your Shakespeare, your Ovid?' Cyrano said it with just the right degree of jaunty sarcasm.

'He writes better than you, and that's for sure!'

'*Really*? I somehow doubt that.'

'Oh, you are good, cousin, but no one puts words together like Christian! He clothes Love in words, like God clothing the birds! No one, no one, *no one* else writes letters like these!' And she rested her hand against her breast so that he knew his letters were lying alongside her heart. His words. His work. His love. It was enough. What better could a man hope for whose nose grew out of his face like a cloak peg out of a wall? What better could a master craftsman hope for than to see his art giving happiness to the madonna he worshipped?

*   *   *

By the time Cyrano caught up with Christian de Neuvillette, he was exultant, his mind full of fireworks. 'Listen! Are you listening? Your theme is Love! So here's what you'll say to her tonight . . . Are you concentrating?'

'I'll do it myself,' Christian said.

Cyrano thought he must have misheard. 'Love, pure and simple. It will be our finest hour! When you begin . . .'

'Save it. I don't need your help any more. I'm grateful, Captain, but . . . well, we've got beyond all that, Roxane and I. I'm not a baby. I know how to take a woman in my arms and tell her I love her. I don't need you holding my hand. Thank you for your help, but . . . from here onwards I'll do this myself.'

And he was gone, running his fingers through his golden hair, squaring his broad shoulders, glancing sideways at his reflection in a brass coach lamp. Cyrano felt like a cigar stubbed out unsmoked, a waiter dismissed with a tray full of uneaten food. The lovely tapestries inside his head hung in tatters. He had outlived his usefulness.

*   *   *

Christian pressed his lips to Roxane's hand and they gazed into one another's eyes. 'Speak to me of Love!' Roxane commanded, already smiling at the prospect of his words.

'I love you.'

There followed a long and unforgettable silence. 'And?'

'I really love you.'

Accustomed to dining nightly on a feast of succulent words, Roxane blinked at him like a hungry chick in the nest. 'Go on.'

'Very much,' said Christian. 'I love you very, very much.'

They were children: she hungry to be loved, he hungry to win her. It was that simple. Why then did they blink and stare at each other in terror. 'Oh, Christian! Open your heart to me!'

'I love you!'

'I know. You said. But you don't . . . say anything else!' Trained up like an orange tree on wires of words, Roxane suddenly wilted without them. She stared at the meagre handful he tossed her and willed them to grow, to put out shoots, to blossom.

'I really do!'

'Do what?'

'Love you!' said Christian in pleading desperation. But though it was perfectly true and his whole soul was pent up in his throat, choking him with passion, he did not *want* to talk about Love. He was frankly sick to death of talking about Love.

He had said everything he found in his head. Couldn't remember what he had said yesterday. Couldn't invent anything new.

Couldn't be bothered, frankly.

Besides, his mouth was too dry with fright and longing. Here she was and here he was. So why was he no longer good enough? Where was his script? Where was his scriptwriter? In the name of Heaven, *where was Cyrano*?

Keyed up and confused, Roxane could not explain the terrible misgiving that reared up inside her, the dreadful disorientation. It was as if the compass inside her was spinning and she could not find north where she had left it the day before. Suddenly Christian was not Christian any more. Absurd to grow angry for want of few pretty and flattering words! Was she really so vain? And yet the more Christian floundered around, throwing those same few words at her *'I love you! I love you very much!'* the more he seemed to shrink, to fade, to lose his brightness. Even his face did not seem as handsome as before. She heard herself, like a spoilt brat, saying hurtful, sulky things.

'Go away! Leave me alone! You don't love me at all! Maybe you've already spent all your words on some other lady!' She knew she was being childish, but somehow, after the fright with the Comte de Guiche, the disappointment got the better of her and she turned and fled indoors.

'Damn!' said Christian with genuine feeling. 'Damn, damn, damn!'

Out of the shadows came the mockery of a slow handclap. 'Oh very good,' said Cyrano. 'Wonderful.'

*   *   *

Roxane no sooner reached her room than a handful of gravel crackled against the windowpane. She went out on to the balcony. 'Oh. You again.'

There was a pause.

'Again and again and again! Like a moth beating itself against a lit window, that's me!'

A warm glow revived Roxane like a sip of brandy. 'What made you so . . . wordless just now?'

Another pause.

'Forgive me, Roxane. For a moment my heart was too full for me to raise it to my lips. But it's there now.'

'Good! Go on!' Another pause. A murmur of voices. 'Is there someone down there with you?'

'No! . . . er . . . No. I was just urging myself to be bold—steeling myself to speak the truth which is . . . pardon? It's what?'

Cyrano gave a gasp of exasperation and pulled Christian aside into the shadows into the 'prompt corner' from which he had been supplying the lines. 'This isn't working,' he hissed. 'Stand aside. We must try something else.'

'Why so halting?' called Roxane, leaning out over the balcony rail, scouring the liquid dark for words, as though for goldfish in a pond. The voice that answered her was strange, strained and deeper than usual.

'In the darkness my words have to grope their way towards you. Yours are falling, but mine have to climb up.'

'I'll come downstairs again.'

'NO! No, don't do that! My words will find their wings presently. Stay where you are. It is perfect this way: you a white summer dress glimmering in the night, me invisible in the shadows, my imperfections hidden. There is no expressing, lady . . . You cannot possibly imagine what this moment means to me.'

For Cyrano found himself speaking his own words, writing his own script, telling of his own love for the woman who stood listening overhead. 'You exist inside me like a bell, so that when I tremble, your name rings through me: *Roxane! Roxane! Roxane!*'

Up on her balcony, Roxane felt a tremor shake her like nothing she had ever experienced. The odd huskiness of the voice below reverberated through her and crazed her childhood into a million shards.

'Believe me, lady. It is the first time I ever truly spoke to you in perfect honesty.'

'I can hear the difference in your voice.'

'That's because the shield of night gives me the courage to be myself, for the first time. I'm sorry if I sound . . . altered. I seem to have strayed into some different world where suddenly

I'm not afraid any more.'

Roxane found she could barely breathe—had to clasp the metal rail of the balcony. The house pitched beneath her; the stars were breaking over her like spray. 'Afraid? You?'

'Yes! I've always been afraid—frightened of being laughed at. So I pretended to be reaching for a flower when really I was reaching for the moon all along—reaching for you, Roxane. If I were to speak my love for you, lady, it would take all the words in the world.'

She was dimly aware that her cheeks were wet with tears. 'No witty banter, then, tonight?'

'None. None. There should never have been any! Passion isn't a fencing match, my love. It isn't about scoring points. Love's a matter of life and death. Love's a rage of sadness and music and desperation. Look up at the stars, Roxane! The distances out there ought to strip away all our arrogance and bluster. Every day we waste life, making light of it, never stopping to look around and see the miracles—

feel the miracles. Oh, Roxane! I pity the man who never meets Love face-to-face and drops his guard and lets it run him through!'

Up on her balcony, Roxane gave a gasp and pressed a hand to her rib cage. Then, to save herself from falling, she had to grip the climbing jasmine that clad the house wall. Below her, Paris was swinging in space like a chandelier ablaze with candles.

'Each time you've looked at me I've become a better man—braver, stronger, more inspired! To see you happy, I'd willingly destroy my own happiness. Do you understand? Finally? You do! I know you do! I can feel it!'

And it was true. Love travelled through the stock and stems of the jasmine, setting the leaves rustling, the tendrils curling, the yellow flowers shedding their pollen. The two of them might as well have been standing palm to palm, their fingertips interlaced. Cyrano pressed his lips to the leaves, and the reek of jasmine filled his head with too much dizzying sweetness. Dew from the flowers fell on to his upturned face. He longed to die, so as never to see this one moment end.

'Why are you trembling, Roxane? God forbid I've made you sad? Have I made you cry? You are weeping!'

Her voice in the darkness was barely audible. 'It's Love, my love. That's all. Love, pure and simple.'

Forgotten, redundant, Christian stood by in the shadows, mesmerized by the flicker of words to and fro. He barely understood what he was hearing (though it made him deeply uneasy). But even he could not mistake the change in Roxane. She fluttered in the dark like a giant white moth, and he wanted to net her. She was crying, and he wanted to taste the salt. She was crying out for something—any fool could see that! and what could it be but him?

Cyrano was saying, 'Looking at you, Roxane, is like gazing into the sun: when I look away again, everywhere is flecked with the scorch marks of you. There's only one thing I ask, and that's . . .'

'. . . a kiss!'

Strands of jasmine broke off in Cyrano's hands. For a few short moments he could not understand where the voice had come from: he had forgotten Christian even existed. Then he turned on the boy angrily. *Be quiet, you fool!'*

'A kiss?' said Roxane. 'Did you ask for a kiss?'

'Yes!'

'No! I forgot myself for a moment. Take no notice. *Christian, get back down here!'* But Christian de Neuvillette had the wind in his tail and was already finding footholds in the jasmine. Cyrano grabbed him by the trouser belt to restrain him. *'Are you mad? Where are you going?'*

'To take what's offered! Time's done for talking! Too much talking!' Christian shook himself free and swarmed up the house wall. He was in no mood to listen to Cyrano (who, in some dark, undefinable way, seemed to have helped himself to the evening). All Christian could think of was taking Roxane in his arms.

Cyrano dared not follow. The great weight of his ugliness held him pinned to the ground like an anchor on the seabed. He drowned in the shadows, watching his rival swim up towards the surface and life and air. Weightless as a flying fish, Christian vaulted over the handrail. Pale hands took hold of his head, his golden curls breaking over and between her fingers.

Cyrano sank his hands in his own hair and pulled so hard that the one pain almost obliterated the other. Christian was right. This was the right and natural progression: from friendship to wooing, from wooing to kissing. And perhaps if Cyrano could dissolve now, like salt, in the darkness, he would not have to witness it. He would not have to stand by while Christian de Neuvillette took from him everything he had ever wanted— helped himself to the moon and ate it like a ripe pear.

'His lips,' Cyrano said under his breath, 'but they'll taste of my words. My words are on his lips. *My words!*'

5

The Man Who Fell Out of the Moon

'Excuse me. Is this Mademoiselle Robineau's house?'

'What?'

It was a monk: brown, tiny, and glisten-eyed, like some small nocturnal animal. 'I have a letter for Mademoiselle Robineau. Is this her house?'

'No. Go away,' Cyrano told him. Had he not vowed that, for the sake of her happiness, he could destroy his own? Well then, Roxane and Christian must not be disturbed in their bliss.

The monk's eyes grew wide with worry, but he turned and started off down the street. 'Oh dear, oh dear, and I have a letter for her from the Comte de Guiche!'

The name fell like shellfire, too dangerous to ignore. Cyrano ran after the monk, recollecting suddenly that Mademoiselle Robineau *did indeed* live at the jasmine-covered house. 'I thought you said Domino, not Robineau.' He spoke loud loudly enough to be heard by the lovers up on the balcony. A man's head and shoulders appeared over the rail. Cyrano feigned astonishment. 'Well! Good evening, Christian! So this is where you've been keeping yourself. I was just passing when I met this excellent object. He has a letter for my cousin, Mademoiselle Robineau!' Tinny and strident, his voice would never be recognized as the one that had lately been speaking out of the jasmine-fragrant shadows.

He could read the annoyance in Christian's stance. Roxane too greeted him frostily: 'Cousin Cyrano?' There was an edge to her voice. A true gentleman would not have embarrassed a lady by standing in the street and hallooing up to her and her lover. But it could not be helped,

68

Cyrano told himself. The Comte de Guiche was mischief: he carried trouble in his wake, as a rat trails fleas. What was he doing sending late-night notes to Roxane?

Fetched down to the street to take the note from the friar, Roxane struggled to make sense of it in the dark. Even when she moved back into the light of the hall, to see better, the words still swarmed across the paper like black beetles. Cyrano moved casually round behind her, so as to read over her shoulder.

The note read:

Divine Madonna,

Despite your tender concern for my good name, I hold fast to my resolve. I will call on you within the hour. How can I depart for war and perchance meet there with my Death without tasting the sweetness of a night with the lady who holds sway over all my affections.

Receive me with kindness. Receive me with openness and generosity. Make sure the maid is out.

I come to you consumed with love and hope.

Your devoted admirer

Antoine

The paper shook between Roxane's fingers. A low growling noise behind her made her glance round and catch Cyrano literally snarling at the letter over her shoulder, his teeth clenched.

At any moment the Comte de Guiche would be arriving here, at the jasmine-covered house, foisting his attentions on her, nuzzling and wheedling, sullying the loveliest night of her life with his mole-black desire. What to do?

Faced with any ambush, her cousin's way was to whip out his rapier and trust to the speed of his swordplay. Well, she too could think and act fast when safety and happiness were at stake. 'Do you know what this note says, Father?' she enquired of the monk, who shook his head till his ears crackled. 'Oh, then shall I read it out to you? It is not very pleasant news to me, I'm afraid.'

The monk gleamed with childlike excitement. Cyrano caught Roxane's eye and smiled: he seemed to be able to read her thoughts.

'This note says (Roxane lied):

Mademoiselle,
His Eminence the Cardinal has expressed the wish to see you married, and soon. In writing to tell you of this, I employ for my postman a most excellent, intelligent, and trustworthy friar.

I realize these plans may not be to your taste, my lady. However, it goes without saying that the Cardinal must be obeyed and that sometimes our personal feelings must be set aside. The young man His

Eminence wishes you to marry is one Baron de Neuvillette, a young cadet currently serving the Company of Guards. (You may be slightly acquainted with him.) So that you may speedily comply, I have sent this Neuvillette under separate cover. He should reach your lodgings at around the same time as this note. Perhaps he is there already. The excellent, devout, reliable and likeable friar will no doubt perform the marriage service without delay. I beg you to brave this ordeal with humility and courage.

I remain your servant, etc. etc.

Antoine, Comte de Guiche

'Oh, but lady!' exclaimed the monk. 'It's after dark! A marriage must be performed within the hours of daylight.

The soonest I can legally . . .'

'Oh look! There's a postscript!' cried Cyrano, peering over Roxane's shoulder and pointing to the bottom of the letter with a gloved finger.

PS. Pray reward my trusty postman with at least 20 gold louis if he carries out the Cardinal's wishes without delay or question.

'Oh!' exclaimed the monk. 'I'm sure candlelight will be perfectly acceptable, so long as there is plenty of it.'

Christian de Neuvillette dashed deeper into the house in search of candelabra, a crucifix, wine, a prayer book containing the marriage service, the bribe money . . .

'How long?' said Cyrano, ushering the monk indoors as if persuading a sheep into a sheep dip. 'How long do you need? To perform this marriage.'

'Oooh, thirty minutes should suffice to—' began the friar.

'Make it quarter of an hour and I'll throw in supper and a bottle of

burgundy to go with the twenty louis.'
At any moment de Guiche's plans
might erupt amid the wedding service,
like a molehill, and sully all Roxane's
happiness. There was not a minute to
lose.

The house was in uproar—Roxane
calling for her maid, Christian calling
for a comb, the bang and scrape of
furniture being moved to form a
makeshift altar. No one heard the
sound except Cyrano, still standing at
the door, half in, half out of the light:
the soft tread of expensive boots on the
flagstones.

De Guiche was already coming.

*　　　*　　　*

Cyrano pelted down the house steps,
wove between the tubs of flowers, and
leapt into the clutches of a tree, pulling
himself high and higher up into its
leafy branches. The twigs snatched at
the brim of his hat, snagged in his
clothing, and jabbed him in the face.
Near the top, one long, sturdy bough
reached out over the pavement. It was

high enough for his purposes, though there was a small chance he would break both ankles when he landed . . .

The man approaching was wearing a mask, but there was no mistaking de Guiche, the fleecy hem of his cloak rippling around his shins like black foam. He was walking fast, leaning forwards, hungry for the delectable Roxane. His route would take him directly under the bough where Cyrano balanced.

Cyrano bent his knees and took several deep breaths. But wait! Would de Guiche recognize his voice? Very probably. Better use a foreign accent English, maybe.

A few paces away, Roxane's house pitched and tossed like a galleon with every porthole a blaze of light. Indoors, in this instant, Christian would be opening his mouth to receive a communion wafer as white as the moon, closing his lips, feeling the wafer soften and disintegrate on his tongue. He was marrying Roxane, swallowing the very moon out of Cyrano's sky and leaving him nothing but the dark. Now

Roxane, swallowing down the wafer, would be speaking her vows, marrying her lover, the darling of her dearest fantasies. Cyrano parted his own lips. Disintegrating on his tongue, like a white wafer, lay the words he had always dreamed of speaking. *I take you, Roxane! Till death and beyond! To be my wife!*

*   *   *

Antoine de Guiche reeled backwards as a huge, yodelling shape hit the ground at his feet and rolled to a standstill.

'Oh! Gad! Bless my soul! By George! Down and not dead! Remarkable! Astonishing! Where am I?'

De Guiche looked upwards. He could see nothing overhead but a full moon in an empty sky. 'Where in blazes did you—'

'From up there, sir, yes, sir! From the moon, sir, as you see—and not a bone broken well, not many anyway. What jolly luck! But *where*, that's what I need to know! Tell me do! Where have I landed? Is it a planet? Which solar system? Or a meteorite? A planetary moon? Where?'

'Out of my way, man! You're deranged! I don't have time to waste on madmen!'

But the Man-from-the-Moon was climbing up him, as though de Guiche was a knotted rope, grasping him from behind, panting down his collar. 'No saying how long I was falling—could have been minutes, could have been three months. One loses track. Bah! Look at me. Covered in cosmic dust. Tufts of solar corona in my spurs . . . My eyes are red raw from astral acid. And these strands from the rear-ends of comets—well, they're worse than dog hairs to get off one's clothing.'

But there *was* no looking at the man, who was still clinging to de Guiche's back. 'Out of my way, I said! I'm in a hurry!' De Guiche dropped his voice to a conspiratorial whisper. 'Look here. I have an appointment with a young lady!'

'Ah! Lovers' meetings? Then where else can I be but in Paris?!' cried the

Man-from-the-Moon triumphantly. 'First rate! How gratifying! Paris is precisely where I took off from!'

Despite himself, de Guiche's curiosity twitched like a shot rabbit. 'You went *up* as well as came *down*?'

'Absolutely! By my own patent method! You don't mind if I just wipe my face on your cloak? I got splashed as I fell through the Milky Way, don't you know. And—ow!—1 thought I had got past unscathed, but do believe the Great Bear took a bite out of my ankle after all.'

'You're either mad or very, very drunk,' snapped de Guiche, trying once more to break free.

'I shall write a book, of course—everyone does these days. I picked up a few dozen very useful small stars just now, to use as asterisks . . .'

'If you think this nonsense is going to . . .'

'That's why I can't reveal the findings of my lunar expedition you do understand, don't you? I realize you're dying to ask me what the moon is made of and whether anything's alive up

78

there . . . but it would simply halve my sales if I were to leak the information ahead of publication.'

De Guiche gave a sob of frustration as the lunatic manhandled him into a plant-pot for a seat and went on bombarding him with nonsense. The fool had his hat pulled halfway down to his chin, so it was still impossible to see his face!

'Of course, you do *know* the four ways, don't you, by which one mounts the astral stairway —I mean the four ways for getting up to the moon?' said the Man-from-the-Moon.

'Four?'

'. . . discounting, of course, that bunk Regiomontanus and Archytas wrote about riding eagles and pigeons and the like.'

Give him his due, he's a very highbrow lunatic, thought the comte. He said: 'I really wish I had time for this, sir, but . . .'

'The First! One constructs a twenty-sided vessel, lines it with mirrors and as the light-rays inside it bounce to and fro among the mirrors, the air becomes

79

refined. And lo, the vessel rises.'

'No!'

'Or . . . the Second! One can strip oneself mother-naked and hang bottles of early morning dew from one's ears, nose, fingers well, anything else that sticks out enough, really. Then, as the sun rises, lifting the dew from the meadows, lawns, etcetera, etcetera, it naturally lifts the bottles, too—though the thread loops can *cut in* a tad . . .'

De Guiche adjusted his clothing, thinking of the discomfort. Then his elbows came to rest on his knees, his chin on his hands, and his eyes glazed as the science fiction tumbled over him.

'I have *seen* the plans for method number three,' said the space traveller. 'A metal grasshopper with spring-loaded thighs triggered by gunpowder . . . but personally I wouldn't risk riding it unless it was built out of best rapier steel. Too much depends on it.'

'Well, yes, I suppose . . .'

'And the Fourth is so simple you must have thought of it yourself long since: the Magnetic Method?'

'Er . . . y-e-e-e-s. Naturally. Just remind me . . .'

'One sits on an iron platform, throws a giant magnet up above one's head; the platform rises to meet it; one throws the magnet again; the platform rises once again . . . and so on *ad infinitum*, as we say in Frinton.'

'So which method did you use?' De Guiche was enthralled. Even the wet earth in the flower tub did nothing to dampen his fascination.

'A Fifth! On the evening of the highest neap tide, I went swimming in the Seine. Still wet, I stretched myself out on the bank, my head towards the rising moon.' He demonstrated, lying down on his back, boots towards de Guiche and hat covering his face. His chest rose and fell like a sea swell and from under the hat came a lifelike imitation of waves breaking against a shore. 'So as the moon rose, plucking and pulling up the tide, the pull also dragged me upward into the sky. Pleasant journey—very smooth until all at once, there was the most tremendous . . .'

From inside the house came a sound of laughter. The door burst open and spilled a lane of light such as the moon lays over the sea. In its path lay the space traveller, a white feather waving in his hatband.

'Yes? Go on?' urged de Guiche, all agog. 'There was the most tremendous . . .'

'Silence,' said the man beneath the hat. 'There was the most tremendous . . . silence.' He uncovered his face, sat up. The English accent was gone; his French was soft and low. 'It's done. Finished. She is married. You are free to go now, Comte de Guiche.'

'Cyrano!?' De Guiche was bewildered. He could see he was the butt of some childish joke, but at first that was all he could see. Then, as bride and groom, friar and maid came out, talking and laughing and celebrating, the Comte realized, little by little, why Cyrano had gone to such lengths to delay him. The woman he thought of as his private property walked on the arm of Christian de Neuvillette.

Prising himself out of the flower tub, de Guiche stalked over to Christian and brought his face close up to his. 'Your regiment is ordered to Arras, boy. Join them.'

'Oh, but, sir . . . !'

'*Join them NOW!* You and your *nose-heavy* captain.'

The bride gave a gasp of horror. 'Antoine! You're not sending him to the war?'

'He's a soldier, isn't he? Where else would I send him . . . unless it's to Hell?'

Panic seized the wedding party: pleas and vows, reproaches, recriminations and goodbyes.

But the real hatred hung leadenly between de Guiche and Cyrano de Bergerac. The comte's top lip rucked and he said: 'I've scotched your little plot, eh, marriage-monger? They may be married but they'll have no wedding night!'

He was surprised by a big, barking laugh that burst from Cyrano. 'Ha! No wedding night! *The fool thinks that causes ME pain!*' he shouted up at the moon, his features exaggerated by the bright, white light.

Through the maze of streets came the insistent beat of snare drums: the regiments were mustering. Cyrano hurried Christian away, lengthening his stride to be the sooner out of reach of Roxane's imploring cries:

'I love you, Christian! Don't go! Go tomorrow! Oh, write to me, Christian! Look after him, Cyrano! Take care of him! Make sure he writes! Promise me he'll write!'

Inside Cyrano his heart slammed over and over again, not so much like a drum but a broken door banging in the wind. 'On my life, lady!' he called over his shoulder. 'On my life!'

6

Easing the Pain

Hunger. It sharpens all the senses, like a razor sharpening a poet's quill. After a fortnight without food, even in the dreary rain and drifting smoke, daylight hurts the eyes. The squeal of rats, the scrape of a blade being sharpened . . . they grate on the ear and on the nerves. The smell of death mixed with the distant cooking fires of the enemy are a double torment. And even a fellow soldier reeling past, dizzy with hunger, inflicts pain with his bony elbows. Nerves are strung out to breaking point.

'Halt! Who goes there!'

*　　　*　　　*

The Siege of Arras went catastrophically wrong. No sooner had the French encircled the city than the Spanish encircled them. The besiegers were besieged. And trapped between the city wall and this hoop of Spanish steel, they skirmished and starved, starved and skirmished. The Company of Guards, under the command of Castel-Jaloux, were all boys of noble Gascon families, raised on pheasant and burgundy. Now they dined on rats and nettles, on sparrows and roots. They pined for Gascony and for their sweethearts and mothers.

Among them was Christian de Neuvillette, pining for Roxane—his almost-wife. His memories of that last night in Paris were a sweet confusion. Now and then a question surfaced slowly through his brain, like a goldfish sipping air. Why had they begun the evening at loggerheads and ended it married? Why had she wept over Cyrano's words? And when Christian got home—if he got home—would she settle for kisses, rather than pretty words? There were practical concerns, too. Where did she want to live? How much did she need as an allowance . . .? He would have liked to write to her and ask, but here he sat, trapped between brick and steel. No mail could possibly get through. Instead, he hid from hunger and longing under a blanket of sleep.

'*Halt! Who goes there!*'

*   *   *

Musket fire from the Spanish lines brought the sentries to their toes, and they peered out into the rainy fields at a disturbance among the wheat. Someone was running, bent double, through the sodden crop, raising a fine spray of water drops, while musket balls shattered the ears of grain to right and left.

'*Don't fire!*' le Bret called to the sentry. '*Don't fire! It's only Cyrano!*' He ran forward as far as he dared, to slap his friend then shower him with insults and reproaches. 'You perfect fool, man! Why must you do it? Where have you been? As if I didn't know. I've been worried sick! Are you wounded?'

'No, no. The Spaniards are getting much better at missing me—I've given them plenty of practice.'

Le Bret clucked like an old turkey. 'The boys are starving; have you fetched us some food at least?'

Cyrano shook the rainwater off his cape. 'I've just been out to the post. I need to travel light.'

'You're a lunatic, you do realize that, don't you? "Out to the post", indeed.' Le Bret knew about Cyrano's forays through the Spanish lines, the insane risks he took, the danger he courted, simply to post a wad of pages, day by day, to the woman waiting in Paris.

'I promised her he would write.'

'Yes, but *every day*?' Running a finger over the front of his friend's jacket, le Bret creamed mud off the woollen cloth. Before dawn each day, to his friend's dismay and despair, Cyrano slipped out of camp and wormed his way along hollow hedges and the furrows of ploughed fields, over dry-stone walls and through bogs. He crept under the very noses of the Spanish

88

troops—crawled through the ashes of their campfires, under the guy ropes of their tents; he borrowed their horses and fought their patrols just to reach some outlying village or a coaching inn and deposit his latest parcel of words. 'Where are you going now?' called le Bret as Cyrano plunged away through the camp.

'To write another letter, of course!' said Cyrano. Finding a soldier asleep in his path he went to step over him, then paused. It was Christian—pale as death but still as beautiful as the seraphim.

'She could always read the old ones!' le Bret called after him, confident of being ignored.

Cyrano replied quietly, so as not to wake the boy: 'If the letters stopped coming she would think harm had come to him. If she only knew . . . The letters are to reassure her as much as anything.'

But it was not true.

He wrote letters as an army surgeon lets blood: to relieve fever, sickness, delirium. Squeezed between Arras and the Spanish, between survival and death, his thoughts built up inside him until he was fit to explode. The only service he could do Roxane was to keep her young husband safe, and yet the boy was starving, along with the rest of the Gascon cadets! Cyrano hated himself for the plight his friends were in.

He hated himself, too, for writing love letters to another man's wife, (even if he did sign them *Christian).* And yet while he could vent the steam of his unrequited love, he could salve his scalded soul just enough to bear the pain. And so every moment he was not scavenging for food, skirmishing with the Spanish, posting letters, or tending the wounded, he sat writing, writing, writing, wearing out a forest of quills, employing an ocean of ink. He wrote so as to fill his head with Roxane and empty his bursting heart of its need for her.

The months he had spent with Christian had made him as fond of the boy as he might have been of a younger brother. In fact he found himself loving Christian on behalf of Roxane, hoarding food scraps for him, checking over his musket, watching his back. Christian's love for his absent wife was dogged and true, and he could not be blamed for his beauty any more than Cyrano could be blamed for being born ugly.

An hour later, le Bret came to find him. 'The boys are in a bad way, Cyrano. Come and put some heart into them. Castel-Jaloux has tried—I've tried, but they can think of nothing but their empty bellies. If the Spanish mounted an attack now, I think ...'

Cyrano seemed to emerge from somewhere far away. 'Today will bring an end, le Bret. I sense it. Either we'll eat or we'll die.' But he rose slowly and walked over to the barn where the cadets were bivouacked.

They looked like so many dead chickens hanging on a butcher's stall— too puny and meatless for anyone to buy. Their eyes, big in their sunken faces, made them look childlike; and, like little boys, they were sulky and whining, in need of their mothers and their mothers' cooking.

'I'm so hungry I could eat my boots.'

'Fillet of shoe-sole—I tried it.'

'I'm so hungry my ears are rumbling.'

'My legs are as weak as the Paris beer. When I try to get up, the world spins around.'

'The world always spins, you fool. Have you only just noticed?' said Cyrano brightly. 'She's trying to throw us off her back into the dark. You just have to hang on all the tighter.'

'I say we should mutiny.'

'Let's eat the generals, at least. They can't taste worse than rat.'

Cyrano could almost see the despair creeping amongst them, like grey mice, nibbling into their frail reserves of strength. He caught the fifer's eye, laid a finger against his own prodigious nose, then began to sing. The fifer took up the familiar Gascon tune.

'Dream, child of mine, where'er tonight you sleep
Of Gascon hills all fleecy white with sheep.

*The cowbells clamour through the
    evening field
And like your eyes the daytime flowers
    are sealed.
The nightingale is singing in a tree
Across the cradling vales of Gascony
And all its songs are lullabies for thee
That wheresoe'er you sleep you dream
    of me.'*

The words trod down their complaints like wet grass. The fife's sweetness pierced them through and through. They sat transfixed, tears forming on their sore eyelids as miraculously as dew.

'Oh, very good, Cyrano,' said Castel-Jaloux reprovingly. 'Now you've reduced them to tears!'

'Just lifting the pain higher, Commander. From their stomachs to their hearts. And if you want to see spirit . . .' Cyrano snatched up a drum and made to signal the alert, but Castel-Jaloux needed no proof of his cadets' courage: he had had plentiful opportunity to see it at work.

In fact it was a volley of Spanish rifle

93

fire that brought the cadets to their feet. A rider was approaching. It was their colonel, the Comte de Guiche, still demon-like in his black cloak, the white lace frothing below his chin like the foam on a rabid dog.

'Look at him,' muttered le Bret. 'At least you can use a peacock to make pens.'

'He's starving too, remember, for all his lace,' said Cyrano mildly, and seeing the surprise on le Bret's face added, 'He's a Gascon like us, when all's said and done.'

Around them, the cadets began to groan and spit at the sight of their colonel whose appearance never seemed to presage anything but bad luck. But Cyrano hissed at them: 'Quick, boys! Suavity in all things! Put on a good show.'

And so, like school children hearing the teacher's steps, they dredged themselves and their belongings up off the floor, crammed on their hats, lit their pipes and *lounged*. They lounged like lizards in hot sunshine, lazily dealing out a pack of cards or reading a book, picking their teeth, crossing their ankles, tossing dice. They were a picture of scruffy nonchalance, so at ease with themselves and so marvellous that a comte wearing Belgian lace and Lucca wool warranted not so much as a bored glance. A law unto themselves, that was the Company of Guards. Smooth as best butter.

Dubiously the comte regarded them down the length of his paper-thin nose. He was not fooled. He knew from personal experience the hunger pangs that were griping at them. They were almost admirable, these wayward Gascons who answered to no one but Castel-Jaloux or the firebrand de Bergerac. Should he praise them, perhaps, or was it too late in the day for that?

'I know what you think of me,' he chose to say, reining in his horse. 'But I find no cause for pride in threadbare jackets and torn trousers. What do you use your panaches for—pipe cleaners? Look at you: no better than scarecrows.'

'I see you're carrying less lace

yourself today, Comte!' observed
Cyrano. 'Where's your scarf of office?
Did you have the bad luck to *lose* it?'

De Guiche looked Cyrano over as
though he were a piece of furniture in
need of re-upholstering. 'As you know
very well, I led a charge yesterday
through the Spanish lines. My scarf
drew attention to my rank and I found
myself the target of a dozen Spanish
blades. So I cast it aside—eh, voilà—I
was anonymous again free to fight a
mere two Spaniards at a time!'

The cadets still gave a low derisive
groan. 'A real Gascon would have
welcomed the extra attention,' said
someone in an undertone.

'I am a Gascon, born and bred!'
retorted de Guiche.

Cyrano seemed unconvinced. 'Surely
not. Gascons are all insane. There's far
too much cold logic in you, sir.'

The comte pursed his lips. 'What
purpose the grand gesture, when one's
men are relying on one?' he said
priggishly.

'The best time for bravado, I'd have
thought . . . Anyway, you could always

have *gone back* for your scarf afterwards.'

De Guiche smiled serenely. 'Then clearly you do not realize how far my charge had broken through. I was *deep* behind enemy lines. My scarf is well and truly lost, but it was lost truly and well!'

'It can't be reached?'

'No more than cheese can be fetched down from the moon, Captain de Bergerac.'

Only then, with a flourish such as a toreador offers a bull, did Cyrano pull something white and lacy from inside his jacket and toss it to de Guiche. It was, of course, the scarf of office. The cadets roared with delight. The comte's bubble was pricked.

To their surprise, the humiliation barely dented his haughty smile. 'I am glad you and your men hold your lives so cheap. No, truly I am! You will regret my news so much less.'

At last the click of dice, the slap of cards, the clink of gambling money fell silent. Le Bret found himself thinking of Cyrano's words: *Today we shall either eat or die.*

*   *   *

De Guiche had spies. Like a spider feeling the vibrations of its web through spread feet, he operated a network of French and Spanish informers. He might not win the war for France, but at least he did not struggle from day to day in blind ignorance. Thanks to a certain Spanish spy in his pay, he knew, for instance, that the Spanish were planning an all-out attempt to break the French hold on Arras. He knew the exact point at which they would attack, too . . . because he had *told* them when and where to do it. With the help of that selfsame Spanish spy, he had advised them to launch a massive attack on the Eastern Gate, held only by a platoon of young yokels: the Company of Guards.

*   *   *

'Time is crucial. It is a diversion, you see, to allow another regiment to break

98

out and reach supplies. I need you Gascons to fight for as long as you are able, and to the last man. You may take it as a compliment, if you like, that I directed the Spanish to attack just here—that I chose the *Gardes Nobles* to make this noble sacrifice.'

Hold the line.

They were to be sandcastles staving off an incoming tide. Bones to keep savage dogs occupied for a while. Matches to fend off the dark. De Guiche was ordering them to die.

He threw the scarf of office round his shoulders and tilted his head in defiant triumph. Cyrano met his eyes. Instantly the scent of jasmine was there in the stinking barn with them, the taste of communion wafers, the murmur of a friar blessing a marriage, a bar of light streaming from an opening door . . .

'And so you have your revenge,' said Cyrano quietly. 'The last resort of a bitter man.'

If hunger is sharp, jealousy is sharper. It gouges the heart out of a man's ribcage. It narrows his field of vision into a single dark tunnel. De Guiche too had loved and lost Roxane. He too needed to vent his sadness and loss, and being without Cyrano's gift of poetry, was reduced to this: to loosing the blackness within him on to Cyrano, Christian, and all the *Gardes Nobles*. Oddly, now it was done, there seemed no lessening of the dark, no relief from the regret. Except that now it was tinged with shame.

'It's true that I bear you no love, Captain,' said de Guiche, 'but my decision was a military one. The courage of the cadets is unequalled and sometimes war calls for martyrs.'

Then Cyrano bowed deeply, sweeping the ground with the plume of his hat. 'In that case, on behalf of the *Gardes* I thank you, Colonel, for the honour of dying gloriously.'

7

Last Post

'Sound the muster! Start building a barricade!

Clear the ground for fighting!' Somewhere a bugle blew and the Company of Cadets sprang into action.

Those puny chickens, too meatless to make broth, were suddenly transformed into musketeers— running, labouring, shouting, swearing, loading muskets, making ready for battle. They voiced no regrets at their fate, except that they must die with empty stomachs: they who could have defeated the Spanish single-handed, given a cartload of rations and a keg of Gascon wine!

Cyrano, having seen to the construction of a barricade five metres high, returned to his solitary corner of camp where, on the tailboard of a broken cart, he wrote all his letters to Roxane. He tore up the one he had begun and spread out fresh paper in front of him. One last letter to write: his letter of farewell.

It did not take long. The words had long since been written inside his head. At the sound of the bugle, the right phrases had mustered inside his head, ready and unafraid.

But such was the height of his love that the looping letters could barely contain it. Such was Love's drag on his heart like the moon dragging on the sea that the ocean of tears inside him over-spilled and splashed the page he was writing. As he reached the end, his quill traced, without his permission, the first letter of his own name.

He stopped himself only just in time.

Oh, to sign it *Cyrano!* To make confession as a dying man makes confession to a priest, leaving his conscience clear. To sign his own letter with his own name!

Now and then, here and there, one of the young men round about him would stop work and stand immobile, feeling Death breathe cold on his neck, brushed by a memory, a regret, a fear. When Cyrano found Christian de Neuvillette, he was standing stock still, arms around his chest, rocking a little to and fro. Cyrano placed a hand on his sleeve.

'Roxane,' said Christian.

'I know.'

'I should write something—all the things I meant to tell her! I wish . . .'

'I thought you might,' said Cyrano peremptorily and reached inside his tunic. The letter he produced was not so large or so elaborate perhaps as the colonel's scarf of office. But it was just as great a proof of Cyrano's bravery.

Too much to hope that Christian would simply fold it away into a pocket—no one's eyes but hers ought to have seen the words it contained. But of course de Neuvillette wanted to read the letter *he* was supposed to have written to his wife; wanted to see what brilliant feathers Cyrano had plucked from the air in order to clothe his own raw, wordless passion.

'I'd have thought you had letters of

your own to write . . .' he murmured, blue eyes flickering to and fro over the lines of writing. Gradually they widened with wonder. 'These things you've said . . . How did you know? How did you even guess . . . ?'

'Oh, we poets, you know,' said Cyrano breezily, pulling used quills from his various pockets and letting them fall so that the wind caught them and carried them flickering away across the muddy ground. 'Something for every eventuality and any occasion. Weddings, funerals, christenings . . .'

And still Christian did not fold the letter away. 'What's this mark? Here in the corner. This circle here.'

Cyrano examined the hangings on his sabre, checked the blade's edge.

'It's a tear stain! You shed tears!' exclaimed Christian accusingly.

A wave of the hand. A casual shrug. 'Well, you know poets. We get carried away. We're like actors: our roles sometimes get the better of us . . .'

'You shed tears!' said Christian again. (Perhaps that letter C standing alone at the foot of the letter reminded him of a man beneath a balcony, body arched with intensity, pressing his lips to the jasmine leaves. Or perhaps he had known all along and simply not chosen to admit it.) 'You love Roxane.'

'It's not death,' babbled Cyrano confusedly. 'That's not so very terrible in itself. But never to see her again that's more than I . . . more than we . . . I mean, more than you could . . .'

'You love Roxane.'

'No! Yes! Of course! Who wouldn't?'

'Loved her all along.'

'But *she* loves *you,* man! You know that! God knows, you've seen it in her—the way she looks at you!'

Doubt stood between them like a third person. The letter blew and fluttered between Christian's gloved fingers. Cyrano went to snatch it back, but Christian crumpled it inside his fist. Perhaps he would have destroyed it but for a sudden confusion of shouts, shots, and astonishment beyond the barricade.

'A coach!' called the sentry. 'Shall we fire on it?'

The coachman, standing up on his

105

foot-board, legs braced, whip in one hand, reins clutched to his chest, was bellowing with all his might, *'In the king's name! In the king's name, make way!'* He had to have driven clear through twenty miles of Spanish-controlled countryside and yet there was no mistaking his French accent.

Antoine de Guiche, already mounted ready to leave the Gascons to their fate, hesitated. His spies had told him nothing of this. 'In the king's name?' What did it mean?

A gap was pulled in the barricade—almost wide enough—and the coach sped through, scattering piles of brushwood and overturning an ammunition crate. Its curtains were drawn and its roof strung with ivy and twigs from careering through woodland. Foam splashed from the horses' nostrils; they were dark with sweat.

'Form a line! Prepare to fire a salute!' cried Castel-Jaloux, unable to guess what grandee or court official had run the gauntlet of the Spanish lines 'in the king's name'.

De Guiche's horse jibbed, uncertain of its rider's wishes. The coach came to a halt. 'You come in service of the king?' he shouted at its closed curtains. Then the door flew open, the steps folded outwards, and the reply came:

'*Yes, in the service of the King of Love!*'

A woman's voice? Like a kiss it astounded four dozen youthful hearts. It brought blushes to the cheeks of fifty hell-raisers who gaped open-mouthed as Roxane Robineau stepped down from the carriage.

Christian de Neuvillette felt his head empty of words and his heart fill with adoration.

De Guiche saw Hell open its jaws to cackle at him. He had just funnelled death and mayhem into this acre of land only to find his love standing at its heart.

Cyrano saw nothing. He was too afraid of what he might feel if he turned and saw Roxane's face again.

Roxane herself was bright and glittering and exultant. She was Cinderella emerging from her pumpkin coach. She made the camp her stage, her arrival a grand entry to rapturous applause. She was just a little too devil-may-care cheerful, tossing aside the war, the Spanish, the danger, like dresses whose colour she had tired of. 'It's time this little siege came to an end, gentlemen! It has really gone on far too long. Ah! There you are, cousin Cyrano!'

Cyrano turned. 'How?' was all he could say. No one knew better than he did the difficulty of breaking through the Spanish lines.

Roxane fluttered her hands. 'Oh, it was easy! Every time we were stopped, I simply said that I was on the way to see my lover! The Spanish are *such* romantics!'

De Guiche darted towards her. 'Yes, but you must get away from here! You must go now, lady! In a few minutes . . . in an hour . . . less . . .'

'Yes, Roxane, you must!' said Cyrano.

Even Christian wanted to silence her brilliant chatter, preferably with kisses. But Roxane was far beyond the reach of reason, drunk on the exhilaration of reaching her destination, achieving her goal. The future had receded to the size of the pupils in Christian's eyes. She was immovable.

The cadets didn't help. They were exultant at the sight of a pretty face. Here was an audience for them to impress. Roxane lent purpose to being brave. So they fetched her a drum to sit on, brushed off their clothes and spat on their boots to polish them. They laughed at her jokes and sighed at the romance of her story.

There was no breaking through to cold reason. Cyrano and de Guiche glanced at each other, like men cut off by the same tide.

'What I would like now is a leg of chicken and a glass of burgundy, if you please, gentlemen!' announced Roxane. The cadets threw up their hands and mopped and mowed like glove puppets, regretting they had nothing to give her, nothing at all. 'Well? What are you waiting for?' she went on. 'Tell my coachman to serve dinner!'

Up till that moment, the only thing anyone had noted about the coachman was his huge Parisian waistline untouched by famine. But as they watched him (apparently) dismantling the coach piece by piece, they did see something faintly familiar about him about his brioche-shaped head, his omelette-coloured hair, his jelly-mould belly, his trifling cherry nose. He smelt sweet too—sweet as in petit-fours and hot chocolate; sweet as in profiteroles and almond tarts.

'Of what are coaches made, sirs?
Of cakes and wine and clementines,
Of oyster soup and cantaloupe,
Of sausages and mutton pies
And galantines—all in disguise.
That's what coaches are made of,
    sirs!'

Bad verse and good cooking. A great shout went up of, 'Ragueneau!' as the poet-pastrycook drew lengths of sausage from the handle of his whip, whole chickens from under his seat, baguettes from his trouser legs, pasties

110

from inside his hat, cheeses from the hubcaps, and a bedroll filled with seventeen assortments of pie. His choux pastry had been reduced to the consistency of volcanic ash and came raining down on twenty upturned faces where it stuck like plaster-of-Paris: death masks of sugar.

Cyrano seized his opportunity. He caught Christian by the wrist and pulled him aside. 'A word.'

'Isn't she marvellous? Have a quail's egg!' said Christian, finally infected by Roxane's feverish excitement.

'About the letters.'

'This one, you mean?' Christian touched the breast of his jacket.

'Hmmm. And the others.'

'Others?'

'You wrote—ah—a little more often than you might suppose.'

'What do you mean? Since we got here, you mean? I wrote? How often?' The grey-brown eyes simply blinked back at him. 'What? Once a month?' The corner of Cyrano's mouth twitched with guilt. 'Once a week?' Cyrano winced. '*Twice* a week? *Three times?*'

'Ah.'

'Bon Dieu! Every day?!'

'Twice sometimes.' Cyrano said it so quietly that Christian thought he must have imagined it.

'Well? So? You couldn't post any of them, could you?'

'Anything's possible.' Quicker than a cough he said it: 'Anyway, if she should mention . . .'

But then the party washed back between them—cadets with mouths full of food and brains soused in wine—and Christian de Neuvillette was left yet again with the feeling that he had been hoodwinked.

He turned and began trying in earnest to persuade Roxane back into her coach. 'What possessed you to come!' he groaned as she resisted every plea.

'You did, of course! Your wonderful letters!' It was not what Christian wanted to hear. 'Oh, my love! Those letters came at me like shooting stars! Like a hail of meteorites! They crazed the moon! They split me into atomies!' (Make her be quiet. Make her stop before she says something that can not be unsaid.) 'Oh, Christian! They scoured me naked! They burned away all that nonsense of looking and wanting and puppy-dog eyes! I saw deep, deep, deep down into you! Those letters—they were your soul speaking to my soul, weren't they? They were the essence of everything that matters between two people who are going to spend their lives together! The things that matter—the things that last!' (Now, when he needed her to be frivolous, she was all too much in earnest. A great calm seemed to invade her.) 'Forehead to forehead looking into each other's souls! Your letters taught me, and I learned, Christian! Oh, I did learn! Every letter you sent opened a window on some new, lovely vista!'

'They were just letters!'

'What you wrote—it's true! Life's a candle burning down. It's lit, it's gone. No more faces, no more kisses, no more glare and flare: just two souls clinging together for eternity. I'll love you for ever, Christian—more than any woman ever loved a man—thanks to those letters!'

'*Don't*! Don't say it! For God's sake—you don't know what you're saying! I don't want to be loved like that! I just want . . . I just wanted . . .'

'What? An adoring silly girl gazing into your blue, blue eyes, hanging on your sleeve? Oh yes!' She laughed out loud at the thought of anything so trivial between them.

'Listen, Roxane! Supposing . . . just suppose . . . in this war . . . supposing I got injured—scarred.'

'Scarred, disfigured what would I care? Oh, I'm *glad* you're so beautiful—God knows, I am—but I'm not in love with your face any more, dearest, or your golden curls or the way your throat . . . No, I could almost wish you *were* ugly, just so that I could prove it to you! It's the man *inside* that I love! The man who wrote those . . .'

Ah, no more about the damned letters! He wanted to cover her mouth with his hand. He wanted to silence her. He wanted to tear in papery shreds the time they had spent apart, the air that

114

separated her mouth from his. And those letters, those damned letters. Breaking away, he pushed and elbowed his way through the press of drunken comrades until he found Cyrano loading muskets behind the barricade. He went at him like a madman, hitting him open-handed about the shoulders and head. 'You and your damned letters! She doesn't love me any more! It's you! It's you she loves! She as good as told me so!'

Cyrano stumbled backwards, taken unawares. No glib response would come; no joke with which to fend off Christian. His heart shrank to the size of a dying star and exploded again in a flash of blinding pain. 'She said that?'

'She said that looks mean nothing. Only souls. Only damned . . .'

Was it possible? Could such things happen, outside dreams? Could a creature so grotesque, so lonely, so loathsome to himself truly win the love of Roxane Robineau?

To add to his confusion, the opening volleys of the Spanish attack instantly broke over the camp like a lightning storm: the deafening crackle of muskets followed by the deep rumble of cannon fire. Cyrano took Christian by the shoulders and tried to hold on until they both grew calmer. 'You're wrong, lad. You must have misunderstood . . .'

But Christian only grabbed his wrist and began to drag him back towards the ruins of the coach. 'Ask her! Ask her yourself, why don't you!'

Buglers were summoning the cadets to arms. It was like wading against the tide to re-cross the camp, but Christian would not let go of Cyrano's wrist. 'I'll be loved for what I am or not at all! Let's find out, shall we, which of us she truly prefers?'

'It will be you! You!' Cyrano protested, trying to wrench his wrist free without actually brawling with Christian.

'The marriage was after dark—no witnesses—no wedding night. It can be undone. It can.'

'But it will be you, Christian! She'll choose you!'

They collided unexpectedly with the

Comte de Guiche. 'Shouldn't the rats have gone by now, Comte?' snarled Cyrano. 'This ship's sinking fast.'

But de Guiche had thrown aside his black cloak, and his black jacket was unfastened, spilling white lace and lawn-cotton. 'The Gascon in me has got the upper hand,' he said, with a grimace. It might almost have been a smile. 'I've decided to stay and fight alongside the Company of Guards.'

A passing cadet stopped and stared at him then ran off shouting, *'De Guiche is staying! The black rat's a Gascon after all!' A* moment later the boy returned with an offering of food for this new-found Gascon hero, but de Guiche sneered contemptuously at the half-chewed chicken leg thrust under his nose: 'I would rather die hungry than eat second-hand food!' he declared, and there were more cries of *'A Gascon! A true Gascon!'*

'Insane after all,' said Cyrano with bemused admiration. And the two men's eyes met a second time. They had more in common, after all, than simply Gascon blood and an imminent appointment with death.

'My spies told me about your daily excursions to the post,' murmured de Guiche. 'And you call *me* insane?'

A sentry shouted that Spanish infantry were advancing through the wheat field. There were snipers in the trees, too, and the Spanish artillerymen were starting to find their range. A shell exploded at the corner of the barn and its roof sagged, loosing an avalanche of burning thatch.

But Christian had finally dragged Cyrano in front of Roxane. 'Cyrano has something important to say to you!' he panted. Then without staying to hear the outcome, he let the tide-race of troopers sweep him back towards the barricades.

'Important?' said Roxane.

'Christian, come back! Not at all, madame. You know what he's like. Always making something out of nothing . . . Roxane—what you said to him just now . . .'

'That I would love him for ever? Doesn't he believe me? Is that what's wrong?' Cyrano swallowed hard. 'Or

118

that I would love him even if . . .'
Confronted with Cyrano's troubled
face, she let the sentence peter out.

'It's all right. You can say it. Even if
he was ugly. Like me.'

She seemed surprised. 'You? Ugly?
You're not ugly, cousin. You're just
Cyrano! But yes! Yes! Even ugly I
would love him! How can a really good
man ever be ugly?'

There was a crack, as if some planet
on the far outskirts of the universe had
broken open and spilled its golden yolk
down the alleyways of Space. Cyrano
did not know whether he had heard it
inside or outside his head. His pupils
contracted and he could not clearly
see. *You're not ugly. You're just Cyrano.*
He could make no sense of the burning
straw around his feet, only that it had
burned away his shadow, the shadow of
his profile.

'What was that noise?' Roxane was
asking.

'Oh, God, Roxane, listen, if what you
say is true, there's something I have to
tell you . . .'

A commotion by the barricades.

Castel-Jaloux calling for assistance.

'About the letters . . . about the whole . . .' said Cyrano.

Le Bret pushing against the throng. His hand on Cyrano's sleeve. His whisper in Cyrano's ear.

At the centre of the universe the Devil laughed shrilly and blew out the sun.

'Yes, Cyrano? What were you going to say?' asked Roxane.

'What? Oh. Nothing. Nothing, nothing, nothing.'

'What happened over yonder? What was that scream?'

'Never mind. Come away, Roxane.'

It was over. A minute before, Happiness had been born to Cyrano like a son. For a moment it had breathed, reached out, touched him, cried. Now it was dead. And nothing can ever breathe life back into the Dead.

The Spanish drums heralded all-out attack. A group of cadets had been trying to carry some unwieldy burden past Roxane, wrapped in a blanket to prevent her seeing it. But they had to set it down now and run back to the barricades as fast as their legs would carry them. Castel-Jaloux had his sabre raised, ready to signal the counter attack. Cyrano was dimly aware that he was neglecting his duty to attend on this woman, this cousin of his. This widow.

As the blanket fell open and Roxane glimpsed Christian's body, she threw herself down on top of him, tugging his hair, ripping open his jacket, searching for his wound like a looter pillaging. She shouted his name in his face: *'Christian!'* Then she turned on Cyrano, her hands pulling at the cuffs of his boots: 'He's alive, Cyrano! He's not dead! Make him live! Say he's not dead!'

And he was not. Though the tiny hole in his jacket was over his heart, it had left Christian de Neuvillette breath and time enough to speak one last word: *'Roxane!'*

It sent her into a frenzied search for water, brandy, wadding, miracles . . . and while she searched, Cyrano swiftly dipped his head close to Christian's.

121

His great nose stirred the softness of that curly blond hair. *'I told her everything, Christian. And it's you she loves,'* he whispered. *'I swear it.'*

Beyond the barricades Castel-Jaloux was shouting commands to the musketeers—*'Load! Ram! Aim! Fire!'* And when the enemy was too close for musketry, there came the order to draw swords.

But in a place as still and black as the heart of a cyclone, Christian let go the smallest of breaths and his blue eyes rolled upwards, as if to some balcony far, far overhead. Roxane, her face pressed to his, felt it grow as chill as candle wax. Her fingers closed on the fabric of his shirt, trying to drag him back into the world of the living: a fold of paper pricked the back of her hand. She drew out the letter: the letter of farewell.

Battle broke up against the barricade like a great wave smashing at a wrecked ship, breaking its back. Frantically Cyrano beckoned Ragueneau from his hiding place under the coach. *'You must get her away! I'm trusting her into your care!'*

But Roxane seemed hardly aware of her surroundings as she gently unfolded the letter, noting the blood that had stained one corner—even the tear stain that had watermarked the page.

'He is dead,' she said incredulously. 'The finest, the most glorious of men.'

'Without a doubt,' said Cyrano.

'All tenderness. All passion. Was there ever a truer lover, cousin?'

'Never, *chère madame*. And you were all in all to him,' said Cyrano.

'He is dead,' she said again and, tasting the truth of it for the first time, fell forward in a faint.

Her head struck Cyrano's breast where he was crouched in front of her. For a moment, his arms closed round her.

So am I, too, he told her in his thoughts, *because now you are lost to me for ever.*

Then he lifted her bodily into the battered coach and slammed shut the door.

8

Blackest Space

There are other things besides Love. It does not occupy every corner of every minute. It does not perch on the door to every room. It does not hang on every coat-hook in the hall. It is not an ingredient of every meal. There are whole books whose pages never touch on it. There are the realms of Nature, Politics, Mathematics, Science. There are other things besides Love.

For a man with an enquiring mind and any kind of genius there is always plenty to do. In any case, to begin with, it took Cyrano de Bergerac all his strength just to stay alive.

*   *   *

At the very height of the battle for the Eastern Gate, a relief force arrived, scouring the Spanish from behind and turning the massacre of the Guards into a last-ditch victory. The relief column found the battleground littered with horses, bodies, wounded men, and what looked like the remnants of a picnic. One officer chanced upon a musketeer captain kneeling by the body of a younger cadet, his forehead on the ground, hands drawn up under his chest. Thinking him distracted with grief for the dead boy, the officer reached down to comfort him but withdrew his hand sharply, covered in blood.

Surviving comrades told how Captain de Bergerac had fought for an hour on the crest of the barricade, with superhuman ferocity, thrashing a hundred Spaniards, until a sabre-cut to his neck had put his sword arm out of use. Fighting on with his left, he had retreated only as far as the body of Christian de Neuvillette where, like an exhausted child falling asleep at its prayers, he had finally knelt down and succumbed to unconsciousness.

*   *   *

The road to recovery was long and tedious. Animals, when they are injured, retreat to a dark corner and lick their wounds. The corner Cyrano chose—a seedy Paris apartment—was lined with books and bottles of ink— enough to keep out the noise of traffic and the tramp of passing platoons bound for the war.

His career as a soldier and swordsman was over. So he sparred on paper instead, with villains and fools and politicians. He wrote plays and stories and poetry. He wrote outrageous, shocking things that made the respectable ladies of Paris fan themselves and protest. He wrote daring, scandalous things that made the gentlemen of Paris guffaw and bluster. He wrote angry, forbidden things that made his enemies grind their teeth and swear to silence him. He wrote to the newspapers. He published pamphlets. Sometimes he wrote about God (though not with any affection). Sometimes he even wrote

127

about sex.

But never about Love.

And when the shadows gathered, like a hundred assassins, in the corners of his dreary little room, he crossed to the windowsill and looked up at the stories scrawled in starlight across the vaults of Space. Cradling his useless sword-arm to his chest like a sleeping child, Cyrano de Bergerac quit the seedy back-streets of Paris and journeyed in his imagination through the pure white landscapes of the moon.

*   *   *

Between whiles, Cyrano de Bergerac went each Saturday to the Convent of the Sisters of the Holy Cross, to visit an old friend.

9

Panache

'Ah, but he is so very *wicked*!' exclaimed Sister Marthe, fitting the top to the pot of marmalade.

'And such a liar!' agreed Sister Claire. 'Last time he was here, he told me he had been to the moon in a cabinet hung all over with firecrackers!'

'And he told me he rode on a white ostrich all over the Sea of Tranquillity!' The two nuns gasped with delighted horror at the enormity of such lies.

'I think he just *might* have been teasing you,' said their Mother Superior gently, 'or talking about some book of his.'

'All the same, I'm afraid he is a *very* bad Catholic,' said Sister Marthe, sounding more excited than regretful. 'You would think, in all his years of coming here, we might have converted him a bit.'

'Oh, we will, we will!' vowed Sister Claire. 'We have to! He's so kind and funny and we all love him so dearly!'

Mother Marguerite held up a hand. 'And I say you won't, you won't. What, and make him think twice before he comes here? Don't torment the poor dear man. You do better making him pots of marmalade.'

'Ah yes! He's so *greedy*!' exclaimed Sister Marthe giggling. 'He never comes here but he boasts how much meat he ate the Friday before. Meat on a fast day! Imagine!'

'The last time he told me that,' said Mother Marguerite, 'I'm perfectly sure he hadn't eaten at all for two days.'

The younger nuns gaped in disbelief. True, Cyrano did not *look* like a glutton. In fact his clothes seemed to billow bigger around him each time he called. And they were always the *same* clothes; always the same shabby clothes. But could the magnificent Captain de Bergerac with all his talk of theatres and balls and banquets and moon rockets really lack for a bite to

130

eat? 'Who told you so, Mother?' asked Sister Marthe.

'His friend, Monsieur le Bret.'

'But don't his friends take care of him? Help him out?'

'He would hate that. He is far too proud ever to accept help. And thanks to his writing, he has more enemies than friends these days. Our captain is not always good at saying the things people want to hear, you know.'

Marthe and Claire looked more disbelieving than ever. After all, Captain Cyrano was the only person who *always* found the right thing to say! He made the nuns laugh and he even knew how to dispel the clouds that hung obstinately over Madame Roxane.

*　　*　　*

For fifteen years, Roxane de Neuvillette had lived within the convent walls. Her widow's black, alongside the nuns' white surplices, made her look like a blackbird among doves. Every Saturday, her cousin

Cyrano visited her, bringing the news, reading his latest manuscript, recounting scurrilous gossip, telling his preposterous tales. They walked in the convent garden, among the whispering leaves, and for a little while Roxane de Neuvillette allowed herself to smile and argue and roundly tell him off for being such a heretic and a ruffian.

Sometimes she even caught herself looking forward eagerly to Saturday and to seeing him. But then she would remember, and gather her sadness round her again like grey knitting wool, and return to mourning her dead husband.

Cyrano was late today. At the sound of footsteps she looked up smiling and ready to chide him for his bad time-keeping. At the sight of the figure in the gateway, a sudden chill went through her that sluiced away fifteen years and filled her nose with the smell of crystallized flowers. The clothes were as sombre as her own widow's black. It might almost have been Death standing there, blocking out the sunlight. Then a black glove lifted from

132

the silver knob of a cane, and the Comte de Guiche bowed as deep as rheumatism would allow.

'Antoine! I had no idea you were in Paris. How good to see you. I thought you were Cyrano.'

'Ah. Yes.' De Guiche, too, had been told he would find the Gascon at the convent.

They walked along the bone-white cloisters, out across the velvety lawns to the cloistering woods where afternoon could only hover like a kestrel above the trees. His cloak, her skirts roused the dead leaves and set them whispering like scandalmongers at the theatre or the prayerful in church. De Guiche spoke of his glittering career on the battlefield, in politics, among the rich and the well born. He noticed that his achievements did not exactly bore Roxane but they did not move her either. She did not covet the wealth or fame he had squirrelled up. Not for the first time, de Guiche discovered that, when he talked about himself, his own words tasted like burned coffee.

Two chairs had been set out under

the trees, in readiness for Cyrano's visit; the cousins liked to sit and watch the moon rise while they talked. Roxane sat down and drew something bright from the pocket of her black dress.

'You have found peace? Here among the little sisters?' asked de Guiche.

'Oh yes! Sometimes this place can seem next-door to Paradise. I am almost there. I can almost sense him, a breath away, just the other side of a wall.'

'So, you still grieve for him. Your Christian.' The old war-wound in his hip gnawed on him like a toothless dog. De Guiche leaned more heavily on his cane, unwilling to sit down for fear he could not get up again with dignity. There was something stubborn, dogged —unnatural—about her mourning a man dead for fifteen years. And yet had he not gone on hankering after Roxane—pointlessly, unrequitedly for the same length of time?

Roxane pulled embroidery threads singly from the tangle in her lap. She looked like an angel mending a

134

rainbow. 'His presence surrounds me . . . like this autumn mist today. I feel . . . how can I explain? as if he is *watching over me.* And I have his letters, of course. All his marvellous letters. Never a day passes but I read what he wrote to me.'

De Guiche turned his face away sharply. There was a long silence, but Roxane was accustomed to silence and read nothing into it. She simply went on tugging at the silken colours.

'And your cousin Cyrano? He will come today?'

'He comes every Saturday, religiously, on the dot of three.'

'Ha! It strains belief to say de Bergerac does anything *religiously.*'

Roxane smiled. 'Oh, I don't believe he's nearly as pagan as he pretends.'

'He has made a great many enemies.'

But still she read nothing into his words: no warning, no hint of danger. 'Dear Cyrano? Nonsense. He's my newspaper—my chronicler. So witty. So cheerful. Nothing ever casts him down!'

De Guiche studied fixedly the silver

top of his cane. *And a consummate actor,* he wanted to say, but did not. Roxane's life was simple: she had simplified it, pared it down to the bare bones of a life. He almost envied her this vacuum, this bell-jar in which she had shut herself up along with her memories and regrets. The nuns—the whole neighbourhood—thought of her as a little saint. De Guiche suspected that saints dressed less often in black than in shabby leathers and white cockades.

All the secrets he knew mustered and squirmed like black eels, but he shook them out of his head, deciding to say nothing. To love Roxane de Neuvillette was to protect her from pain, to preserve her illusions and her sad, shadowy, peaceful existence here among the convent willows.

'Ah! Here comes Cyrano at last,' said Roxane hearing footsteps. 'No, no! It's not! Goodness! I am blessed with visitors today.'

De Guiche hastened through the trees to intercept le Bret and take him by the sleeve. 'Have you seen Cyrano today?' he asked in a low whisper. 'No?'

Le Bret looked old and tired and harassed. He drew away slightly from his old commanding officer, as if fearing a trick. 'Isn't he here? I thought he would be here. This is Saturday, isn't it? He never misses . . .'

'When you see him, give him a message from me,' whispered de Guiche. 'Tell him to take care. I heard a rumour today. He's given offence once too often, so I hear. There was talk of him *meeting with an accident.*'

Le Bret stared back at him, blinking, slow-witted and afraid, as if one burden too many had finally been laid on his shoulders. But they were within earshot of Roxane now, and there was nothing to be said. De Guiche pinned on a smile and raised his voice. 'And how is that old rogue de Bergerac these days?'

Le Bret gnawed on his lip and clutched his hat to his stomach. He seemed glad of the chance to blurt out: 'Oh, he's not well! Not at all well! Every time I see him his belt's pulled one hole tighter! And his great nose has turned the colour of wax!'

Roxane laughed lightly. 'Oh, le Bret! How you poets do love to exaggerate!'

Le Bret looked up pleadingly into de Guiche's face as if hopeful at last of being believed. 'He's down to his last suit of clothes and he goes to bed at nightfall for want of a dinner to eat or candles to work by!'

He wilted visibly as de Guiche waved a hand airily in front of his face, as if to disperse the smell of pity. 'These things happen.'

De Guiche felt the man's hatred like spittle in his face. He shook his head. His tone was gentle. 'You think me callous—heartless—malicious, even. But you're wrong. It's true: I have everything: wealth, rank, influence, renown . . . And yet. And yet . . . De Bergerac is richer in the things that truly matter. He has stayed true to himself. He's preserved his *integrity*. He's never settled for half-truths or second-best—never fawned on the rich for the sake of a hand-out. He's never lied or flattered or changed his opinion to curry popularity; never kept silent to save his own skin. He's never slandered a man behind his back. He's never backed down in an argument or surrendered in a fight. Pity him, le Bret? I don't pity Cyrano de Bergerac. I envy him a life well lived. And I'd be proud to shake his hand, if ever I was man enough to do it.' He clasped le Bret's hand instead, and the thought of life's griefs and injustices made their eyes drift back to Roxane untangling her rainbow of silks.

They left her there, awaiting her cousin: 'so witty, so cheerful', and never cast down.

Four o'clock came, and with it the closing of windows and doors. Five o'clock came and Parisians began to turn home from their work carrying their bread and fruit, their private joys and troubles.

'It seems Captain Cyrano won't come today,' said Sister Marthe, anxious despite herself.

'He'll come,' said Roxane, winding scarlet thread around the fingers of her left hand. 'Cyrano always comes.'

And he did.

At six o'clock, just as the convent gates were about to close for the night, he arrived like some storm-wracked pirate ship limping into port, its sails in rags, its rigging shot away, its hull listing and holed. His hat was crammed down so far that his face hardly showed.

Roxane did not look up, so she did not see what hardship it cost him to walk the length of the convent garden and reach his chair under the trees. 'What time do you call this, cousin?' she said gently, smiling down at her embroidery.

'Regrets, lady. I was delayed, damn it. A very tiresome, persistent visitor. I told him: *I'm sorry, this is Saturday. I have a long-term appointment that cannot be broken. Come back in an hour or so.*'

'He will just have to wait,' said Roxane. 'I shan't let you go until sunset at the earliest.'

He lowered himself into his chair, gripped the arms, closed his eyes. 'It may have to be a little earlier than that.'

Sister Marthe, joyful in her role as bringer of marmalade, came gliding demurely through the trees. Her eyes were dutifully downcast, but she could not resist darting a glance at Cyrano as she bent to place the jar by his chair just to check the truth of what the Mother Superior had said. She caught her breath. The face below the big musketeer hat was ashy white, its eyes sunken like hot coals into snow. A dribble of blood was following the contours of eye-socket and cheek, as if loitering in the shadows of his gigantic nose. 'Hush. It's nothing,' he whispered, his eyes flicking in the direction of Roxane.

'Come to the kitchen later. There's hot soup . . . Promise you will come!'

And he did promise—which frightened Sister Marthe even more because he never usually did anything he was told. 'What, am I out of character tonight?' he teased, seeing her anxiety. 'Well then, how else shall I shock you, little Marthe? I shall say . . .' His voice dropped again to a whisper. 'Pray for me in the chapel tonight.'

This time the bashfulness left her and she met his gaze square on. 'I didn't realize I needed permission, monsieur,' she murmured and fluttered away like the dove from Noah's Ark in search of firm ground. The trees shivered, and a handful of blood-red leaves drifted rockingly to the ground. Such courage—to launch themselves on one last beautiful downward excursion, despite the rot and decay that lay in store for them in the wormy earth.

'Well?' said Roxane. 'And now you are here, am I not to have my weekly entertainment?'

Cyrano sat up a little straighter. 'Of course! Of course. I am remiss. Let me see now. Last Saturday the king got an upset stomach after eating too much gooseberry fool. The gooseberry bush was hanged at dawn for high treason. At the Royal Ball seven hundred and sixty-three white wax candles were burned to death in the name of merriment. On Sunday news came— yet again—that we are on the point of a glorious victory that will end the war once and for all—I make that the fourth time this month. Madame d'Athis's dog needed a sedative. Nothing much happened on Monday, except that Lygdamire fell in love. On Tuesday the whole court moved to Fontainebleau Palace and Lygdamire fell out of love again. On Wednesday the Lady Mancini thought she was all set to become queen. On Thursday she found out she wasn't the only one up for the role: in fact the king was holding auditions. On Friday Molière stole an entire scene from my play and put it into his—barely changed a word: well, they do say theft is the sincerest form of flattery. And on—'

Without warning, he slumped sideways in his chair, his hands jerking in his lap, his head rolling forward on to his chest. Roxane gave a cry and threw herself on her knees beside the chair. She called for help, but the bell was ringing for vespers and it drowned out her words.

It did not matter. In a moment, his eyes opened and, after a moment's confusion, he reached up and tugged his hat securely into place. 'It's nothing,' he said. 'I'm all right. Just the old wound from Arras, you know? Sometimes . . .'

He touched the scar on his neck, and she in turn laid her hand to her breast. 'Ah yes. We both carry a wound, don't we, that never quite heals? Mine's here. The ink fades, but not the pain.' And so once more Roxane withdrew from the Real World into a sentimental Past as simple and perfect and tragic as the Garden of Eden.

'You said I might it read it one day: that letter of his,' said Cyrano.

She was delighted—as if he had expressed an interest in her embroidery or asked after her mother. 'Oh, would you?'

'Today I want to very much, yes.'

The letter hung in a silk bag, on a cord around her neck, where the religious might carry a holy relic; where the superstitious might carry a lucky charm. Roxane drew it out with infinite tenderness; even so its folds were fluffy and split from over-much handling. In one corner was a bloodstain the size of a red wax seal; in another, a tearstain. She handed it to him, and Cyrano looked down at his own handwriting, as familiar as his face in a mirror—more so, since he shunned mirrors. Roxane returned to her chair.

'Goodbye, Roxane. Soon I am going to die.'

'Aloud?' She had not been expecting that, had not expected the words to fall on her like the blood-red leaves.

'I think Death will come today, and my heart is so full that it spills over at my eyes. It rages, too, knowing that never again will I see myself reflected in your eyes; that mine will close on your beauty while others go on seeing it. I try to recall them—all those tiny instances of beauty I celebrate each day in my heart: how you brush your hair back from your eyes, or dip your lids when you laugh . . .'

'The way you read it!' Roxane's sewing slid from her lap. The breath tangled in her throat and myriad colours exploded behind her eyes.

'All the parallel lines of the universe meet in you, my Infinity. All the great-circles of the world were formed to cradle

145

you. The sun draws its heat from my passion. The moon is pale with longing, on my behalf. And must I never see you again?'

'That voice!' The scent of jasmine buffeted Roxane, though there was no jasmine in the convent garden. The arms of her chair were metal filigree entwined with vine; a balcony rail. From the hill where they sat she could see Paris spread out like a maze clogged with darkness. Lamps were being lit. The sky was perforated with bats. Only in the west was there some remnant of the sun: a blood-red stain fading in one corner of the sky.

Under the convent trees it was far too dark to read. The letter, in any case, hung from his fingers close by the grass: a white moth drowning in dew. And still Cyrano spoke its contents.

'All these years I have plied you with words, but words are black and white and my skill is not equal to my love. My love has need of colours never seen and words never coined. Aeons of time and even the edgeless universe are not room enough to hold it. I know at least that

146

Death is too small to snuff it out, and that tomorrow and tomorrow and tomorrow it will still fill the sky above you and hide in the hollow of your hand, undiminished and unending.'

'And for fifteen years you have acted out the role of the old friend who calls round to be witty and entertaining.'

Her voice fetched Cyrano back from some faraway time and place. He snatched up the letter.

'It was you,' said Roxane. 'It was you all along.'

'No! I promise you, no!'

'Your voice in the darkness.'

'No, Roxane! You're wrong!'

'Your letters.'

'No! I swear!' Like a prisoner under torture he protested his innocence. 'I never loved you! It was Christian who loved you!'

'You love me.'

In his desperation to make her believe him, he took her hands between his and pressed them to his lips over and over again. 'No! No, my dearest love! My only love! My beloved Roxane! I never loved you.'

147

Somewhere a roosting bird dislodged a dead twig that sighed through the leaves and hit the ground with a dull crack.

'But why? What was the need?' said Roxane, dimly aware that the hands she was holding were icy, icy cold. 'Why lay waste to fifteen years? Why couldn't you just have said: *those are my tearstains on that letter of yours*?'

He brandished the crumpled paper between their faces and said very clearly and deliberately: 'Because it was his blood!'

The moon, rising through the branches of the trees, looked pocked and scarred and deathly white. There was a clamour at the convent gate: fists rattling the wrought iron and the tinny scrape of the bolt.

Roxane understood him. She could see now how perfectly in character it was for Cyrano to have kept silent: to have sacrificed his own joy for the sake of another's memory. Always generous to a fault. Always the noble gesture carried through to the point of folly. She curled up at his feet and laid her head in his lap. The moving, mercury moonlight gradually silvered over the garden, trees, path, chairs, the white panache in his hatband, and re-awoke in Roxane the possibility of joy. Even if all those years had gone to waste, the mistake had at last been righted, and there was time in hand for happiness. There was time. 'It's not too late,' she said.

Then the peace of the garden was shattered and like chain-shot the great mass of Ragueneau came crashing through the trees, shouting, 'He's here, I know it! Is he? The dear fool! With a hurt like that? Did he come here? How did he get here? I knew he would! I knew he'd come here!' His face was gleaming with syrup and sweat and tears, for he had run all the way from his kitchen, weeping aloud at the news his poet friends had brought him.

A deep, mirthless laugh shook Cyrano. 'Ah yes. Forgive me, lady. I never reached the end of my weekly chronicle, did I?' With immense difficulty he rose to his feet, the better to make his grandiose gestures. 'On

Saturday the twenty-sixth, on his way to an appointment with a lady, Monsieur Hercule-Savinien Cyrano de Bergerac —poet, dueller, philosopher, space-traveller, soldier, musician, and general figure of fun—was ambushed in a dark alley, by a lackey who brained him from behind with a block of wood.' He removed his hat, and Roxane could see where his scalp had been gashed open, where his hair and collar were sodden with blood. 'How appropriate! How in keeping with the rest of my life! I had thought at least to die on someone's sword point, my weapon in my hand. But even my death is like something out of a farce. Ugly and ridiculous. Just like me.'

'*Sister Marthe! Sister Claire! Come quickly!* Don't move! I'll fetch help!'

But sinking back into his chair, he caught hold of her skirts. 'Don't go, Roxane. I wouldn't be here when you got back.'

Roxane looked at her hands. A moment before, they had been full of silver. Now the moon went behind a cloud and they were empty again. 'I should have given you everything. And all I ever gave you was unhappiness,' she said.

'No! No.' He stroked the cloth of her dress with his fingertips. 'That's not true. You gave me friendship. Other women looked at me and laughed. Not you. You at least looked beyond my face. And the friendship of a woman is a great blessing—oh, a very great blessing!'

The moon came out again and lit a dark trickle of liquid as it crawled down his brow. It was as if the angels had leaned out of heaven to anoint a dying man with blood. Cyrano looked up and, with a wave of his hand, acknowledged the moon like an acquaintance glimpsed across a crowded theatre. 'Ah! There's that other friend of mine. He wants me. I am going to have to leave you. That's where I'll go now. Up towards his light. Maybe up there I'll find an alternative Paradise made for free-thinkers. What do you say? A rational Paradise peopled with philosophers and poets and men of principle—other exiles like me!'

'Please live,' begged Roxane. 'I love you!'

Cyrano hesitated for a moment, his head on one side, as if waiting for something. Then he gave the smallest of smiles. 'No. You see the magic fails. When Beauty says "I love you", the Beast should be transformed into a handsome prince. But I stay just the same.'

Roxane pressed her lips to his temple. 'I only ever loved one man. And I have lost him twice over.'

'Hush, woman! Don't mourn less for Christian,' he scolded her. 'He was a good man, and he loved you the best he could. But if, when the cold washes me away, you could mourn for me a little while, too . . .'

Roxane could not even cry. It was as if the moon had scorched her eyes dry of tears.

As for Cyrano, his eyes had always seen more than the simple surface of things. Now they began to see things invisible to the living. Into the garden came Death, his grinning skull lacking any size or shape of nose. And at his back came the hundred various assassins who had bedevilled Cyrano's life since first he had buckled on a sword: Untruth—Injustice—Hypocrisy—Cant—Bigotry—Corruption—Compromise . . . They lurked and leered and honed their blades razor-sharp against stone-white thigh bones. Though his feet weighed like stone and his hands seemed gloved in lead, he stood up and drew his sword. The ground heaved under him like the sea.

Roxane and Ragueneau made to support him, but he shook them off. 'No! No one help me. No one! I'll do this alone. I've faced worse odds!' And with one hand against the trunk of a chestnut tree, he began to wield his sword in wild and whirling arcs. 'In the end you'll defeat me, I know,' he taunted the shadowy demons, 'but at least I'll go down fighting!' His voice was as thin as the wisps of night mist that ragged the treetops. His face was a mask of pain. 'And when tonight I bow with a flourish at Heaven's gate, I shall be able to present something worth the giving! Something that outlasts this mean, tallow life—and outshines it too!'

His sword, pointing at the moon, flashed brilliantly as it fell from his grasp. Then he too pitched to the ground.

Roxane cradled his head in her arms and kissed him on the mouth, thinking him dead already. 'What, my love? You didn't say what! What will you present at the gates of Heaven?'

But his eyes opened once more and he smiled triumphantly, tasting the words on his lips before he spoke them: 'My . . . *panache*!'

And the trees, white in the moonlight, swashing in the rising wind, took up the word, as warriors take up a fallen hero:

Panache! Panache! Panache!